WITHDRAWN

I've travelled the world twice over,
Met the famous: saints and sinners,
Poets and artists, kings and queens,
Old stars and hopeful beginners,
I've been where no-one's been before,
Learned secrets from writers and cooks
All with one library ticket
To the wonderful world of books.

© JANICE JAMES.

ONLY OUR LOVE

Returning to Hartfield after her father's death, Linda found she needed to establish new relationships with at least two members of this strong-willed, exasperating, lovable family. Luke Ferndale was all too ready to organise her life. Angus, his grandson, missed in Linda the sparkle she'd had as a child. It took a taste of gaiety and luxury, experience of independence and loneliness to make Linda sure when capitulation was no weakness but both joyful and right.

Books by Iris Bromige
in the Ulverscroft Large Print Series:

THE ENCHANTED GARDEN
THE HOUSE OF CONFLICT
GAY INTRUDER
COME LOVE, COME HOPE
ROUGH WEATHER
THE BROKEN BOUGH
THE STEPDAUGHTER
THE QUIET HILLS
AN APRIL GIRL
THE TANGLED WOOD
A SHELTERING TREE
A MAGIC PLACE
THE BEND IN THE RIVER
THE NIGHT OF THE PARTY
ROSEVEAN
LAURIAN VALE
THE YOUNG ROMANTIC
A HAUNTED LANDSCAPE
A DISTANT SONG
ALEX AND THE RAYNHAMS
STAY BUT TILL TOMORROW
A HOUSE WITHOUT LOVE
THE PATHS OF SUMMER
THE HAPPY FORTRESS
OLD LOVE'S DOMAIN
THE NEW OWNER
ONLY OUR LOVE

IRIS BROMIGE

ONLY OUR LOVE

Complete and Unabridged

ULVERSCROFT
Leicester

First published in Great Britain in 1968 by
Hodder & Stoughton Ltd.,
London

First Large Print Edition
published November 1985
by arrangement with
Hodder & Stoughton Ltd.,
London

British Library CIP Data

Bromige, Iris
    Only our love.—Large print ed.—
    Ulverscroft large print series: romance
    I. Title
    823′.914[F]   PR6052.R572

    ISBN 0-7089-1373-3

Published by
F. A. Thorpe (Publishing) Ltd.
Anstey, Leicestershire
Set by Rowland Phototypesetting Ltd.
Bury St. Edmunds, Suffolk
Printed and bound in Great Britain by
T. J. Press (Padstow) Ltd., Padstow, Cornwall

Only our love hath no decay;
This no tomorrow hath, nor
  yesterday,
Running it never runs from us away,
But truly keeps his first, last,
  everlasting day.
              John Donne, *The Anniversary*

Contents

Love is
a time of enchantment:
in it all days are fair and all fields
green. Youth is blest by it,
old age made benign: the eyes of love see
roses blooming in December,
and sunshine through rain. Verily
is the time of true-love
a time of enchantment—and
Oh! how eager is woman
to be bewitched!

1

Return to Hartfield

OUTSIDE the train window, primroses were blooming on the embankment and the golden catkins of the hazel trees tossed in the March wind. It was a cold, bright day, with cumulus clouds billowing across a blue sky and the wind too keen for the first tender veil of green on the hawthorn. So often, thought Linda, nature seemed to keep her harshest treatment for the first delicate blossoms and leaves of spring. A glimpse of rooks busy about their nests at the top of a group of elm trees reminded her of the rookery at Hartfield, and took her back over the years to the time when she and her parents had been frequent visitors there. She wondered whether she would find the house changed, or recognise the surrounding countryside of meadow and stream, coppice and sunken, twisting lanes, as the enchanted land of her childhood.

She opened her handbag and drew out the letter to read again.

My dear Linda,

News of your father's death reached me yesterday. You have my deepest sympathy.

It is many years since we met, but, as you know, your mother was a very dear friend, and I am only sorry that circumstances have prevented us from seeing you since her death.

I should be so glad if you could come and stay at Hartfield for a week at Easter so that we can renew our acquaintance. My son and his family will be joining me for the holiday weekend, and I know he will be as glad to see you again as I shall be. My grandson will also be here for a day or two.

Shall we say the eleven-fifteen train from Victoria on Thursday morning next? If this is agreeable to you, Martin will meet you at Lynwood Station, and I shall look forward to a very happy Easter reunion.

Yours sincerely,
Luke Ferndale

2

Luke Ferndale, known to her as Uncle Luke, she remembered as a rather alarming man with abundant grey hair and piercing eyes, massive in build and abrupt in manner. She had always escaped from his presence as soon as she could to explore the delights of the extensive grounds of the house, hoping to find Amos, the gardener, whom she adored. Was he there still, she wondered, and would he remember the child who pestered him with so many questions and helped him with more zeal than skill?

A feeling of disloyalty to her father had made her hesitate to accept the invitation, and even now, as she folded the sheet of notepaper and put it back in her handbag, she was not quite easy in her mind about her decision. Her father had disliked Luke Ferndale and had severed all connection with the Ferndale family after the death of her mother, when he moved from the district to Cornwall. If he had heard from the Ferndales since, he had said nothing to her about it. The letter had come as a great surprise, and for a moment she had wondered who Luke Ferndale was, so much had happened in the years between.

The train had reached Ellarton, the largest town in that area. Here the carriage emptied and the train continued on the branch line linking several small country stations along the valley until it came to an end at Lynwood. Walking up the draughty, narrow wooden stairs of that station, she emerged into the lane to see two cars waiting. Almost immediately, a chauffeur emerged from the large black car and came up to her.

"Miss Dawley?"

"Yes. You're Martin. I didn't recognise you."

"Nor I you, miss. You had a pigtail when I last saw you."

She remembered him now. A dark, quiet-spoken man whose wife was the housekeeper. They lived in what had been called the stable flat although cars had replaced horses long since.

The village of Edenmere was some fifteen miles from Lynwood, and by reason of the narrow, twisting lanes which approached it and its remoteness from the railway, had remained largely unchanged, so that the drive was like a journey into her childhood.

"It's still just as peaceful and lovely. I hadn't expected that," she said.

"Aye. We've been lucky. These lanes were only intended for horses and traps," added Martin as he brushed the hedge to allow a small van to pass.

Over the humped bridge across the stream, then the right turn up a lane cut out from steep banks covered with ferns and overhung by arching beech trees whose gnarled roots writhed like snakes on the banks each side. Bare now, the trees filtered the sunshine in a flickering pattern. In summer, the lane would be a green tunnel. She remembered the delicious coolness of it one hot day when she and her father and Angus Ferndale had come blackberrying. They had seen an adder, she remembered, coiled on a stone, asleep, and her father had written a little verse about it afterwards.

Down now into the valley and round by an ash tree through a wide gateway with the name Hartfield on the right-hand stone pillar. A shiver ran through her as the car moved along the gravelled drive. Her father's ghost protesting? The large grey stone house, stark but imposing, offered no reassurance.

It was Harriet Ferndale, Luke's daughter, who came into the hall to greet her. It was she who had been mistress of the house ever since Linda could remember. Ten years had made little difference to her appearance. Linda remembered her as a sallow, serious woman, unapproachable by a rather shy child. Now she looked a little thinner, and her black hair was streaked with grey. Otherwise it was the same Miss Ferndale of her memory who gave her a long, appraising look and said, without smiling:

"Linda Dawley. And the living image of your mother."

"And you haven't changed at all," said Linda with a smile.

There was a wry little twist to Harriet Ferndale's mouth as she said:

"Things don't change much here. Come along into the drawing-room. Father's waiting for you there."

In the drawing-room, Luke Ferndale stood with his back to the fire, hands clasped behind his back, but here time had left its mark on the picture of her memory. The stoop of the broad shoulders, the deep furrows between nostrils and mouth, the sparse white hair, the network of lines round the eyes, all adjusted the picture; but a powerful, intimidating presence still. There was a pregnant silence before she went to him with outstretched hand.

"Hullo, Mr. Ferndale. It's a long time since we met."

He took her hand in his and scrutinised her gravely. She had the strange feeling that in some way he was shocked. Then a smile broke his grim façade and he said:

"Not by my wish. Welcome to Hartfield again, my dear. For a moment, I thought it was your mother as I first knew her. The likeness is uncanny. I never saw it when you were a schoolgirl. At least, only in snatches. Now . . . Well, I'm very happy to have you here again, Linda. Over tea, you shall tell me all about yourself. It will be here in ten minutes. Harriet will show you to your room now. I hope you'll be comfortable."

To her surprise, Harriet did not join them for tea, which was wheeled in on a trolley by a maid.

"You shall do the honours," he said, as he sank in the armchair opposite her. "No sugar and very little milk for me."

She felt nervous as she poured the tea under his watching eyes, and began hastily to talk about the countryside which had delighted her on the drive from the station.

"You're a country-lover, like your mother."

"And my father," said Linda quietly.

"And tell me how you liked being buried away in such a remote spot in Cornwall."

Linda found this difficult to answer. The cottage, quite isolated in a valley about a mile from the sea, was primitive although picturesque, and there had never been enough money to make it really comfortable in winter. And for all her love of the country, her isolation had sometimes weighed heavily.

"In fine weather, it was glorious. In the winter, it could be bleak."

"H'm. Your father never had any success with his writing."

"Poetry, which was his real love, is never successful commercially. We managed on what he earned from his country articles and children's books. Living was cheap there. We grew our own vegetables and had poultry. We were almost self-supporting."

She saw him looking at her work-roughened hands, and she dropped them on her lap beneath the level of the trolley, out of his vision. Her hand-knitted jumper and cheap skirt she could not hide, and her head lifted a little defiantly as she met his gaze.

"What happened to your schooling?"

"I went by bicycle and bus to the nearest school until I was sixteen. Then I left, because my father's health was deteriorating and he needed care."

"And now?"

"We rented the cottage. Our tenancy agreement was on a monthly basis. I'm leaving at the end of next month. I'm looking for some sort of living-in job."

"You've no money? Forgive me for asking all these questions, Linda, but your mother was a very dear friend and I am your godfather. I promised her to do what I could for you. A promise which your father made it impossible for me to keep. We won't go into that. But I feel I have a right, as your godfather, to know how you stand now that you're left alone."

"You don't have to worry about me, Mr. Ferndale. I've enough money to pay the rent for the cottage until the end of next month, and I expect to have a job to go to then." In fact, it had taken almost all the spare money she possessed to pay the return fare from Cornwall and the previous night's hotel bill, and she was banking on finding a job quickly after this week at Hartfield.

"I may be able to help you there. I have a lot of contacts. Anything particular in mind?"

"Well, I can type. I typed all my father's work. I can keep house. I can garden. I'm afraid that's the extent of my qualifications to earn a living."

"We'll think about that. Meanwhile, you must have a good holiday here before you start work. You've had a very unhappy time, my dear, with all the nursing of your father and his death, and nobody to help you shoulder the painful duties. I only wish I'd known sooner. Your father would never have allowed me to help you, but we might have managed something quietly between us."

"I would never have concealed anything from him. We were happy together, Mr. Ferndale. I wouldn't want you to draw any other conclusions from what I've said."

"Well, may I hope that you'll allow me to do what I can to see that your life is a little easier now?"

"It's kind of you to invite me for a week's holiday. I'm grateful and I'm sure I shall enjoy it. May we leave it at that?"

"Your mother's gentle manner and your father's confounded pride. I don't think any the less of you for that, Linda, or for your loyalty. I think, and hope, we can be friends. I'm a plain-spoken man. I don't beat about the bush. But the past has woven a tie between you and me which I would like to see strengthened. All I ask of you is that you should meet me without prejudice, in spite of your father's attitude. Am I asking too much?"

"I shouldn't have come if you were."

"A good answer. I like you. You're honest, like your mother. Hope you'll get on well with the family. You remember my son, Austin, and my grandson, Angus, no doubt."

"Yes."

"Austin married again. His wife died, you may remember, a few months before your mother. That was an unhappy year. Austin's second wife brought him a

11

stepson, Roland, who is your age and married to a pretty little girl, Angela. They'll all be arriving tomorrow, except Angus. He can't be here until Monday. Austin and his wife and stepson live in Bermuda, running a hotel I bought."

"And Angus? He joined your business, I expect."

"No. My grandson chose to be an accountant and is now in practice in the City. I see little of him. We ought to feel honoured by his presence this week-end."

The old man's voice was dry and it was apparent that Angus was not favoured. He went on briskly:

"And now, my dear, I expect you're tired after all the travelling, and would like to unpack and find your way about. Don't hesitate to let Harriet know if there is anything you want. Dinner is at seven-thirty."

He rang the bell for the maid, and, feeling dismissed, Linda gave him a quick smile and went up to her room. It looked out over the garden, and she sat down on the window seat, searching for old familiar features in the garden she had loved, a little bewildered by all that had happened recently. The life which she had known for the past ten years had crumpled with her father's death, and this sudden transposition to the scene of her childhood and that very different life when her mother was alive made her feel that time was playing strange tricks on her and she could not get her bearings.

The part of the garden in view had changed very little: the copper-beech on the lawn, massive, its leaf-buds swelling, cast a moving pattern across the grass as the wind stirred its branches, and dominated its surroundings still. Along the fringe of the woodland belt beyond, the same daffodils danced in the wind and the same wood anemones looked like white confetti among them. The yew hedge on the left of the lawn was thicker and taller now, and one of the group of three cherry trees had been cut down. When they were in bloom, they had looked bridal, but this Easter, an early one, their buds were still tight and they would not be wearing white for Eastertide.

She looked round her room, warm, spacious, comfortable. The whole ground floor of the cottage would have fitted into it. The white door opposite her led into a bathroom as large as her cottage bedroom. Had she been wise to come here? She felt out of her element. She possessed hardly any clothes fit to be seen, had no money and an inborn reluctance to play Cinderella and evoke pity. Her life had been hard and lonely, but she had been happy with her father and their life together had possessed a quality not to be bartered for comfort. And yet, Mr. Ferndale was her godfather, it was kind of him to invite her here and to offer help, and he and her mother had been old friends. Why did she feel a sense of betrayal? An uneasiness? And the gaucherie due to the solitary life which she had led did not help her.

Pushing introspection aside, she began to unpack, smiling at the paucity of her wardrobe and the dimensions of the furniture to accommodate it. If she put one garment in each of the drawers, she still could not muster enough to go round, and her one dress and coat looked decidedly lonely among the long row of coat-hangers in the wardrobe which occupied almost the whole of one wall. The mirror did not reassure her. In this house, she felt

14

dwarfed. It was not a pleasant feeling. She chided herself for this morbid mood. It was probably because she was tired after the harrowing events of the past weeks. For the first time in years, she was facing comfort, a holiday without chores. Whatever unhappiness lay in her heart, whatever the uncertainties of the future, it would be foolish and wrong-headed not to make up her mind to enjoy it.

Running the bath water, which was piping hot, she scattered bath salts with reckless abandon from the glass jar on the window ledge.

In the drawing-room below, Harriet eyed her father with some curiosity.

"Well?" she asked cryptically.

"Well what?" he replied impatiently. He was standing by the window, his shoulders hunched, staring out across the garden. Harriet lit a cigarette and leaned back in the armchair.

"What do you think of your godchild now that she's grown up?"

"As I expected; sacrificed on the altar of her father's so-called artistic sensibilities, as his wife was. That child's had the

minimum of education and has led the life
of a peasant, from what I can gather,
looking after him. Now he's left her penni-
less, quite unequipped for life either
socially or in any other way."

"She didn't have to stick it, once she'd
come of age."

"She has her mother's sense of duty, and
Dawley had charm and knew how to play
on people's sympathy. The helpless artistic
temperament that has to be cherished and
protected. In reality, a selfish failure,
without the guts to acknowledge his failure
and set to and make a decent living to
support his wife and child. Dawley always
made me sick. Now I see that he sacrificed
his daughter as well as his wife to his
egotism, I . . . Well, the chap's dead, and
the girl's young enough to retrieve her life
with a little help."

"Your help?"

"Certainly. She's my godchild, and I
promised her mother I'd look after her. I
regret now that I didn't make more determined efforts to get through to her. I just
despised that man so much that I couldn't
trust myself to see him."

16

"You're a good hater, Father," said Harriet, half mockingly.

"Not hate. I don't like that word. Just anger that helpless women with too strong a sense of duty and service should be used by a man so callously. A man who called himself a poet, who thought he had more delicate sensibilities than the rest of us and was entitled to be cherished accordingly."

"Righteous wrath, in fact."

"Sarcasm is not becoming to a woman, Harriet. It's a habit I've noticed growing on you."

"Sorry. I didn't think so badly of Stuart Dawley myself. A chip on his shoulder because his work wasn't a success, but he certainly had charm."

"And used it to serve his own ends."

"Well, what do you intend to do for the girl?"

"Get to know her a bit better first. Then help her to find a decent job, if that's possible with her lack of qualifications and experience."

"You could make one for her, I've no doubt."

"That has never been my way, Harriet, and you know it. I believe in helping people to help themselves. Not doling out charity. I shall have to give the matter a good deal of thought. Meanwhile, see that the girl has everything she wants to give her an enjoyable holiday. Heaven knows, she's earned one!"

"Yes. Whether she'll enjoy it, of course, is another matter."

"Why shouldn't she?"

Harriet shrugged her shoulders.

"Can't see her fitting in with the family very well. A bit awkward, I thought. Out of her depth."

"She was nervous. So would you be if you'd just emerged from a prison. Try to make her feel at home. I wish you wouldn't smoke so much, Harriet. So bad for you."

He left her and she smiled wryly as she flicked the ash off her cigarette and leaned back in the chair again. He was annoyed with her because she knew too much. She thought they had finished with the Dawley affair. Now Stuart Dawley's death had brought the daughter back into their lives. She might have known her father hadn't forgotten and wondered how he had heard about the death. He had ways of keeping himself informed, the old fox. It would be amusing to see how the family reacted. Linda Dawley, looking so like the woman her father had loved. It had all the makings of a sour comedy.

2

Encounters in a garden

AUSTIN FERNDALE and his family arrived at Hartfield just before lunch the next day and Linda was introduced to them over sherry.

"You remember Linda, Aunt Diana's daughter, Austin. Well, here she is after all these years," said Luke, leading Linda forward.

Austin, a tall, dark, pleasant-looking man, deeply tanned, with greying hair, shook hands and gave her an affable smile. His wife, Cynthia, fair, beautifully dressed and with a well-poised charm which Linda envied, echoed her husband's pleasure. Her son, Roland, and his wife, Angela, nodded over their sherry, and Luke went on to explain to Angela:

"Linda's mother was a very close friend of the family, and Linda is my godchild. She's been living in Cornwall for the past ten years, so we've rather lost touch. Now we're glad to have found her again."

"Cornwall. Such a fascinating county. Were you anywhere near Lamorna?" asked Cynthia, who had a charming voice to go with her looks.

Jumping at this lead eagerly, Linda was able to relax and talk about the country she knew so well, feeling grateful to this second Mrs. Ferndale for her tact and ease. The first Mrs. Ferndale, she remembered, had been a lively, disconcerting person; a good tennis player who had coached her once or twice in those far-off days.

"Is Angus coming, after all?" asked Austin.

"I made a special point of asking him, and he agreed to join us on Monday for the day," said Luke drily.

"Then we'll be having our business meeting on Monday, I suppose, since that's the only day we'll all be here."

"Oh, I don't think we'll mix business with pleasure," said Luke affably. "This is, after all, a holiday, and I don't often have all my family assembled together under my roof."

"But I thought . . ." began Cynthia, then stopped.

"What, my dear?" asked Luke.

"That you were going to tie the men up with business matters and that we females would have to amuse ourselves," said Cynthia gaily. "I'm glad that you've changed your mind, father-in-law. I like my menfolk to relax at holiday time and give us some attention."

"You never lack that, Cynthia, I'm sure," said Harriet.

"She's got the best business head of any of us," said Austin, laying a hand on his wife's shoulder. "What I should do without her at the hotel, I shudder to think."

"Silly," replied Cynthia, smiling at him. "I only look friendly and soothe ruffled feelings behind the scenes and in front."

"And a very valuable service in running a hotel, my dear," said Luke gallantly.

"Well, shall we tell the head of the family our good news, Angela?" said Cynthia.

"Bless the woman!" exclaimed Roland. "She's only been in the house ten minutes and she can't wait any longer to proclaim that she's going to be a grandmother. I'm amazed that you're so eager to take on a role that you look far too young for, Mother."

"Well, this is happy news, Angela, my dear," said Luke. "We can do with some young additions to our circle, and Angus shows no signs of wishing to marry and raise a family. When I was his age, I already had a son and a daughter. When can we expect the new Henlow?"

"In September," said Angela, and did not sound over-enthusiastic about it.

She was exceptionally pretty, thought Linda, this young wife of Roland's, with her ash-blonde hair and large grey eyes, her apple-blossom skin and petite figure. She tucked her hand under Roland's arm now as though for support, and he smiled down at her. They made an appealing picture, for Roland had inherited his mother's fair colouring and good features.

"Very wise to start your family while you're both young. I'm delighted. The nicest Easter egg you could have brought me," said Luke, and offered his arm to Cynthia as the gong sounded for lunch.

Harriet observed this piece of old-fashioned courtesy with an enigmatic smile and shepherded the rest of the family into the dining-room. Linda, placed between Luke and Austin Ferndale, said little while talk ranged over the Caythorpe Hotel in Bermuda and a certain engineering group which Luke considered a good investment. As far as she was concerned they might have been talking about planets in outer space.

Although Linda could not but warm to old Mr. Ferndale's efforts to make her enjoy her visit, she was conscious of a certain strain during the next two days, for it seemed to her that she was under scrutiny from the rest of the company, in spite of their amiable manner towards her. There were undercurrents, she felt. Then wondered if her solitary life had made her too imaginative. At all events, they showed no lack of interest in her.

Seeking to escape alone into the garden on the Saturday afternoon, Roland followed her and joined her on the seat in the orchard.

"The sun's quite warm here," he said. "That yew hedge cuts off the wind. Think I'll join you for a quiet smoke. You don't, do you?"

"No, thank you."

"From what Aunt Harriet tells me, I must just have missed knowing you when you used to come here. I first met old Mr. Ferndale nine years ago, and it was about then that you moved away to Cornwall, wasn't it?"

"Ten years ago, soon after my mother died."

"I remember being tremendously impressed with Hartfield when I first saw it. I was sixteen, and it was way above my experience of homes. I was a pretty awful snob then, I remember. A year later, my mother married into the Ferndale family and I became part of the establishment, so to speak."

"Were you pleased?"

"Naturally," he said, laughing. "A wealthy family with this sort of background for my mother, who'd had a pretty meagre time since my father died when I was at prep school. I like my stepfather, and I've a great admiration for old Mr. Ferndale. Haven't you?"

"Yes, but I don't really know him. I don't know any of the Ferndales except through the eyes of the child I was. I left here when I was fourteen."

"Still, you must have enjoyed coming to Hartfield. You almost grew up here, I gather."

"Oh no. That's an exaggeration. I came here often with my mother. We lived quite near, in a cottage at Rushleigh. I loved this garden. And we used to have jolly tennis parties. Angus and his mother were both very good players."

"How did you get on with Angus?"

"Either splendidly, or the reverse. He was seven years older than I was, and although the gap didn't seem to matter so much at first, he grew right away from me once he went to Oxford."

"Which was his undoing, according to his grandfather. They don't hit it off at all, you know."

Linda pulled a piece of long grass and twisted it in her fingers. She was uncomfortable at this talk. It seemed distasteful to be sitting here discussing everybody.

"They had one final and glorious row when old Mr. Ferndale at last digested the incredible fact that Angus was not going to work for him in any capacity whatever," went on Roland. "He would never have sold the family business if Angus had agreed to go into it. As it was, he sold out for a packet, I can tell you. A bit rough on my stepfather, who had no say in it, but he was never a keen business man, anyway, and Mother says he's far happier running this hotel."

"How long have you been there? In Bermuda, I mean."

"Mr. Ferndale bought the hotel about six years ago, more as a hobby to provide him with an interest in his retirement, I think, though my stepfather was not at all happy with the service agreement the old man had organised for him with the company he sold his business to, so it was a sort of consolation prize for him. He jumped at the chance to get out of industry into the luxury hotel line, I can tell you. And so say all of us."

"It must be grand to live in a country with so much sunshine."

"Yes. You had a pretty bleak time in Cornwall, I guess. Not much of a life for a young girl. I suppose you were jolly glad to get in touch with Mr. Ferndale again."

"It was a complete surprise when he wrote to me. I'm afraid I hadn't given him a thought for years."

"He wrote to you, did he? How did he know where you were?"

"I haven't an idea," said Linda coolly, growing tired of this inquisition.

"Oh well, I suppose we shall have the usual sword-play when Angus gets here on Monday. Must say I wish his lordship would remove himself altogether, although I suppose that would hardly be politic. He doesn't like us, you know. My mother and me. Resented his father marrying again, most likely. Quite understandable, in the circumstances. He's always agreeable enough with us, of course. But underneath the smooth surface, the steel, if you know what I mean."

And women were reputed to be the biggest gossips, thought Linda, studying the handsome profile of this talkative young man. Perhaps he sensed her criticism, for he turned and gave her a charming smile as he said:

"All this in confidence, of course. Wouldn't normally rattle the family skeletons like this, but just wanted to put you in the picture. You seem a bit lost."

"I've been locked away in Cornwall for a long time," she said lightly.

"Not to worry," he said, patting her on the shoulder. "Mr. Ferndale means to look after you now he's found you again, Aunt Harriet says. And he's a decent old boy, if you keep on the right side of him. At seventy-eight, I guess he's entitled to be humoured. That grandson of his should have more consideration for his age. Oh, hullo, darling. Feel better for your nap?"

"Yes, thanks," said Angela. "I wondered where you were. It's a bit chilly for sitting around, isn't it?"

"Fairly protected here."

"I'll never get used to this climate after Bermuda."

"Poor little puss. Like me to take you for a drive before tea? It'll be warm in the car, anyway."

"Yes, let's."

"Care to come with us, Linda?" asked Roland.

"No, I'm going to look for the gardener. He's an old friend of mine. Thank you, all the same."

They went off, and Linda was about to proceed to the vegetable garden to see if Amos was there when Cynthia Ferndale came round the yew hedge and exclaimed with pleasure as she saw her.

"Ah, there you are, Linda, dear. Have you seen my children?"

"Roland and Angela? Yes, they've just gone off to the garage. They're going for a drive before tea."

"Very nice, too. The country's looking so beautiful here now. What a nice sunny retreat you've found! May I join you for a few minutes?"

"Of course."

"I expect this place is full of nostalgic memories for you," said Cynthia. "But perhaps nostalgia is not the right word to apply to a girl of what? Twenty-odd?"

"Twenty-four."

"Yes, definitely too young for nostalgia. That only afflicts one after the mid-thirties. Still, pleasant memories, I'm sure."

"Yes."

"Were you here a lot when you were a child?"

Here it comes, thought Linda humorously. Anyone might think she was a spy and they were trying to crack her false identity.

"Yes. My parents and the Ferndales were old friends."

"How old were you when you first came to Hartfield?"

"I can't remember. A babe in arms, probably. I only know that this garden was my playground for as long as my memory goes back."

"And my father-in-law is your godfather, and yet I never even knew of your existence. Austin did, of course, but he'd forgotten you. How nice for you and my father-in-law to have come together again! He's obviously very fond of you."

"Well, we really hardly know each other. I found him something of an ogre when I was a child. But a kind ogre."

"Of course. Bless him, he does have a rather unbending personality. But pure gold underneath. A fine, upright old gentleman, if ever there was one. I'm sure he's not going to let you go now that he's found you again."

"I have to find a job. It may take me anywhere."

31

"Oh, I'm sure Mr. Ferndale will find you an opening. Hasn't he said so?"

"We haven't discussed anything in detail."

"Well, you've come to the right person for help, dear."

It didn't seem worth pointing out again that she hadn't come, that she had been sent for, so she merely gave Cynthia a polite smile and made no reply.

"There's no warmth in this sun," said Cynthia, getting to her feet and buttoning up the jacket of her pale blue tweed suit. "I shall have to go back to the fire and keep Harriet company."

She smiled graciously and walked away, her high heeled shoes making progress difficult through the long grass of the orchard. Linda stayed on the seat for a few minutes, watching the daffodils swaying in the wind, reminded of the wild daffodils which grew in such abundance in a Cornish valley. The buds on the apple trees were swelling. The flickering chequered pattern of sunshine and shadow across the grass beneath the trees was reassuring in its beauty. Almost reluctantly, now, she left it to look for Amos. She feared that he, too, might seem a stranger after all these years.

It was with an experienced eye now that she admired the trimly-kept vegetable garden, with its seed beds presenting a wonderfully fine tilth, ready for the spring sowing. At first she did not see him, then a movement behind the greenhouse drew her attention to the small figure of a man hoeing between the rows of broccoli. In her childish eyes, he had always looked old and wrinkled, and as he turned she saw delightedly that he looked just the same: thin, brown as a wizened nut, and surely that was the same pair of brown corduroy trousers and the same mud-coloured felt hat. He was frowning at her, leaning on his hoe.

"Hullo, Amos. Don't you remember me? Linda Dawley," she said as she went up to him, smiling.

"God bless my soul! So it is." He pushed the felt hat back farther on his head as though to get a better look at her, then added, "Lindey Lou, who fed the hedgehog and asked so many questions. A quaint little soul, you was."

And when she heard the soft burr of his

33

Dorset voice, the years melted away and she felt really at home for the first time since her arrival.

"You haven't changed a bit, Amos. I was so glad when Mr. Ferndale said you were still here."

"Aye. Me and this garden belong. Shan't be parted till I die."

"You taught me a lot. I had to look after our garden in Cornwall. Only a small one compared with this, of course, but I grew all the vegetables and fruit we needed, and a lot of your tips came in useful. The sort you don't get in books."

"Aye. A ha'porth of experience is worth a ton of print. Well, I must get on, but it's right good to see you, lassie. Spring's a busy time, as you know. Nature's on the move, and she moves fast. I've a job to keep up with her."

"You don't have any help?"

"Help? Worse than a plague of greenfly, the sort you get now. No, I want none of them in my garden."

"Can I help, then? I've an hour to spare before tea."

"The same Lindey. I missed them big brown eyes of yours when you went, and the way you used to trot round after me no matter what I was doing. Funny little lass, you was."

"I'm better able to help now. Try me."

He studied her with the cornflower-blue eyes which were so unexpectedly vivid in his dried-up face. She remembered these silences while he weighed things up. He had no small talk, and was always sparing of words.

"If you'd like to mow the grass paths between the beds, I can get on with sowing my lettuce and carrot seed. The mower's in the shed there."

Linda smiled as she went to fetch the mower. It would take a lot to convince Amos that she could be trusted with anything more skilful than mowing or weeding. It was an old-fashioned push mower which he kept for the narrow paths between the vegetable beds. He grew his vegetables in separate small beds instead of the usual large and dull rectangular bed, and some whimsy had made him shape them roughly to correspond with the shape of the vegetable grown, so that the small round bed had grown beetroots, the large round bed, cabbages, and a triangular bed grew carrots. It had amused her when she was a child to guess which vegetable seed went where, but now she could appreciate the common sense behind the scheme, for smaller beds were much easier to tend and were accessible from all sides, which eliminated much trampling of the soil. It was a practice which she had followed herself, but she had never achieved the artistic shapes of Amos's beds. Happily, now, she trundled the mower round them while Amos marked out his drills and sowed his seed as though performing a sacred act of devotion, which, in a way, he was.

It was not until Mrs. Martin appeared with a cup of tea for Amos that Linda realised the time and reluctantly left him to his kingdom.

3

Angus

THE river ran fast over its shallow bed of pebbles, glinting in the sunlight. Linda leaned on the little stone bridge and watched it. The water was clear and she could see minnows darting about, and now and again the shadowy forms of larger fish. The soft chuckle of the water, the warm sun on her head and the pleasing pattern of the bare trees on the river banks induced in her a mood of tranquil content. She needed this hour alone. She remembered seeing a kingfisher here once, and being entranced with the flash of blue and chestnut as it vanished upstream. Some celandines on the bank near by were glowing richly gold, their flowers open wide to the sun. England in spring, she thought. Was anywhere more beautiful?

A dark shadow half under the bridge caught her eye and she leaned farther forward over the low parapet to see what it was. Surely not a fish, that size? It moved in the eddies of the water, projecting and receding. Her eyes returned to the river banks. The first slight film of green was showing on the hawthorns, and a group of willow trees trailing their graceful fronds over the water looked golden in the sunshine. But her attention was drawn back to the shadow under the bridge. Like an unexplained tapping on a window, it teased her. She would have to find out.

Immediately beneath her was a flat, shallow rock. A small drop from the bridge brought her on to it. She stooped down, peering at the shadow and saw that it was nothing more significant than the branch of a tree caught up in some weed.

"What is it?"

She jumped at the voice and looked up to see a dark face that was familiar. She knew him instantly.

"Only the branch of a tree."

"Looked like a pike, but the water's too shallow. Want a hand up or are you staying there?"

"I'd like a hand. This rock's not as comfortable as the bridge."

She put one foot on the bottom ridge of

the parapet. Without his help, she reflected, she would have had to paddle out, for the gap was larger than she had realised. He took her hand.

"Right," he said, and gave a firm pull.

She grasped the bridge with her free hand as she came up, and as she steadied herself, he took her under the shoulders and she scrambled over the parapet beside him.

"It's Angus, isn't it?"

He looked at her, surprised, then said: "Great Scott! Is it Linda Dawley? Of course. I can see now. At fourteen, you looked a bit different," he added smiling.

"Well, you don't. I knew you at once."

His dark face was thinner than she remembered, but the mocking eyes could have belonged to nobody else, nor the deep, slightly husky voice.

"Aunt Harriet told me that Grandfather had winkled you out from Cornwall, but it had slipped my mind. I was sorry to hear about your father. I liked him. He was always marvellous about country matters. Wild flowers and birds."

"Yes. He loved nature. He turned away from the world after Mother died. I think he felt it had no use for him and he had no use for it."

"Did you like it in Cornwall?"

"It was beautiful, but sometimes cruel, too. We were a mile from the sea, but the coast there was stark and the cliffs high and steep. I really prefer this kinder sort of country."

"Life hasn't been too easy for you, I guess," he said and she was conscious of his scrutiny as they leaned on the bridge side by side.

"I wouldn't say that. You got here earlier than you were expected, Angus."

"I haven't presented myself yet. I stopped the car down the lane and thought I'd have a stroll along the river first. When I saw you go over the bridge, I wondered what you were up to. Not suicide in barely a foot of water."

"We came fishing here once, remember?"

"Yes. And we saw a kingfisher."

She turned to him, pleased.

"You remember, too. I've never forgotten it. One of those enchanted moments."

"M'm. We ended up on a less idyllic

40

note. It turned out that you only liked fishing as long as I caught no fish. When I caught a trout, you thought it was cruel and threw it back. We had a furious row, and that was the end of our fishing expeditions."

That had marked the end of their companionship, too, she thought. He had been seventeen and no longer wanted a ten-year-old child tagging along. Before then, he had been kind and friendly, although his moods varied and she had sometimes found his teasing hard to bear. After that, he became a stranger and she saw less and less of him. He had sometimes turned up at the tennis parties with a pretty girl. Usually a different one from the last, but all attractive. And there had been none of the old friendly communion between them again until the last time she had seen him, on the day of her mother's funeral. Until that moment, she had forgotten it, but now a little picture sprang vividly to life from the past. It had been a wet day, and she remembered the churchyard and the long rain-sodden grass she had stumbled through after the others had left, to find Uncle Luke still there, standing bare-headed at the foot of the grave, just looking. Something in the attitude of that still figure had sent her away, blinded with tears which joined the raindrops streaming off her wet hair, and she had blundered into Angus, hanging about outside, and had cried on his shoulder. The other cars had gone. Only Uncle Luke's car, with Martin patiently waiting, remained. It was barely ten minutes walk from the church to their cottage. Angus had taken her arm when she had recovered a little, and they had walked back together, in silence. But she had been comforted by his presence.

"Do you find the place changed after all these years?" he asked.

"Yes, and no. It's an odd experience, coming back to the scene of your childhood after ten years in which you've grown up. People are the same, yet different. I hadn't heard about your father's second marriage, of course."

"I'm seldom here. Hartfield doesn't change much but my family has changed all right. I guess things never were quite what they seemed to you, though."

"Well, at least Amos is the same. He's

unchangeable, like the sea. And to him, I'm still Lindey Lou."

"Lindey Lou. Yes, I remember. It suited you. You were a funny kid: pigtail, brace on your teeth and wide expectant eyes, as though round the next bush something wonderful was waiting."

"Well, to Amos I'm still the same."

"No pigtail, no brace, and far less expectant."

She had a feeling that he found the change for the worse, and said quickly: "And you, Angus. You're an accountant in practice, so Mr. Ferndale told me. You live in London?"

"Yes. In a flat. I get away at week-ends, though."

His tone did not invite more questioning, and they relapsed into silence, watching the water below them, until he straightened up and said:

"Well, I suppose I'd better put in an appearance at Hartfield. Can I give you a lift back, or are you out for the morning?"

"I think I'll walk back along the river, thank you, Angus."

"See you later, then."

He nodded and walked off. He had

always moved well, she remembered, watching him, and had never gone through the gangling stage of youth. Tall, lithe, and with an almost lazy elegance of movement which had been so deceptive on the tennis court, where he had infuriated her by piling up points with seemingly little effort while she had raced about like a demented greyhound to small avail. Not an easy person to know, she thought. But none of the Ferndales were easy to know.

Alone in her room before lunch, she looked at herself in the mirror, thinking of Angus's critical scrutiny. Her reflection looked woefully plain when she thought of the beautiful poise of the second Mrs. Ferndale and the fragile beauty of Angela. In her solitary life in Cornwall, she had given little thought to her looks. Now, the shabbiness of her clothes was brought home to her by contrast with the others and she found little that was reassuring in the thin face with its brown eyes and the chestnut hair that had all too obviously been cut without skill. But more than anything, it was the sense of inadequacy, of uncertainty, that bothered her. She lacked all confidence in this setting, which had once been so familiar to her, and she wished she could throw off this Cinderella mood, which her father would condemn as a foolish bowing to conventional standards. That he was too rigid and bitter in his rejection of worldly standards, she had come to realise in the past few years, although she shared to a great extent his sense of values. But life was for living and she wanted to embrace it in all its aspects, and not shrink from it. Yet, instinctively, she did shrink from it. She felt so ill-equipped. And she envied Angus his superb assurance.

4

Question of a will

"HULLO, Aunt Harriet. Where are you off to with such a purposeful air?" asked Angus.

"Only going to the post."

"I'll come with you. How's life with you?"

"Much as usual. You haven't quarrelled with your grandfather already, have you?"

"No. We've had a polite little session together, and he is now discussing the hotel with my father and Cynthia. Roland started pumping me about Linda Dawley, so I did my evaporating trick."

"Yes, he's tried me, too. Why he thinks I know more than Austin, I can't think. He and Cynthia go sniffing round like a couple of hounds. You ran into Linda on the way here, didn't you say?"

"Yes. We had a chat. She's changed a lot. I feel sorry for her."

"She won't thank you for that. People don't like pity."

"She looks half-starved. And quenched, somehow."

"You'd look quenched if you'd been living in poverty and isolation in a primitive cottage in Cornwall. The more fool her for staying there. Easy enough for a girl to earn a decent living these days. It was more difficult when I was young."

"Are you regretting that you never forsook the path of duty and kicked over the traces, then, Aunt Harriet?" asked Angus, amused.

"Do you think it's been all that exciting, keeping house for your grandfather?"

"Oh, I don't know. You can't compare it with Linda Dawley's life. After all, you've never had to do the chores. There's always been plenty of money, and staff. You could have had your independence any time."

"That's all you know, young man. Anyway, I'm not discussing the past with you. Your generation has had it easy. You wouldn't understand. That girl's grown so like her mother that it gives me a start every time I see her."

"Like Aunt Diana? Yes, I suppose so,

but Linda's mother was such a gay person. Linda was always a sensitive, thoughtful kid. She could be fun, though, then. Now she seems a bit dim."

The same velvety brown eyes, thought Harriet. The same oval face and lilting voice. Linda's hair was not quite so bright as her mother's, which had been copper-coloured, but she had her mother's slender figure. She lacked the vitality, the strong personality of her mother, though. This girl was unsure of herself. Diana Dawley had never been that.

"You look grim, Aunt Harriet," went on Angus. "Family gathering too much for you?"

"Not at all. I'm getting a good deal of quiet amusement out of it, as a matter of fact."

Angus glanced at her and grinned. They had always got on well, he and Aunt Harriet.

"I bet you are. I gather that Grandpa's cried off the business talk this gathering was supposed to be in aid of. That's set Cynthia's nose twitching. And Roland's, too."

"A little more respect in your references

to your stepmother would do no harm, young man."

"Come off it, Aunt Harriet. You and I don't have to pretend."

His aunt eyed him severely, then a faint smile softened her tight mouth as she met his dancing eyes. She shook her head at him and posted her letter in the box at the corner of the lane, making no comment.

"And here comes one of the hounds," said Angus, as they turned to walk back. "I must say Roland's persistent, if nothing else."

"Hullo, there," said Roland when he was in speaking distance. "I was hoping for the chance of a quiet word with you two."

"What about?" asked Angus blandly.

"The old gentleman changing his mind about that business talk. Father's livid about it, especially as Mr. Ferndale's given no reason."

"Grandfather doesn't confide in me, as you well know," said Angus shortly, for even after eight years, it still jolted him to hear Roland use the term Father.

"Has he said anything to you, Aunt Harriet?"

"Why should he? You know he always keeps his own counsel about his affairs."

"Yes, but he did tell us that he had decided that the time had come to make a new will, and that before giving instructions to his solicitor, he'd like to tell us what he proposed to do. Now he's suddenly side-stepped the whole thing. There must be a reason."

"Why worry?" asked Angus smoothly.

"Oh, I'm not worried, but while we're over here on leave, it's a good opportunity to let us know his plans and wishes. It's very inconvenient for all of us to be away from the hotel together, and we were given to understand that it was because he wanted to discuss his will. After all, he's got to face the fact that he's not young any more and make provision for the future if the tax vultures aren't to confiscate nearly all he's got in death duties."

"Father will enlighten you all in his own good time," said Harriet.

"But time isn't on his side."

"Isn't it? He's extremely healthy and may well live another ten years or more. Now you two had better get a move on if you want to wash your hands before lunch.

You know how my father hates unpunctuality. You won't want to earn a black mark, Roland," concluded Harriet.

It was impossible to miss the sting in the last few words, and Roland frowned as he closed the front door behind them. Harriet left them and disappeared in the direction of the kitchen.

"Your aunt doesn't grow any sweeter with age, Angus. Typical warped spinster."

Angus went ahead up the stairs without comment.

5

Turning point

WITH the sudden change of weather so characteristic of the English climate, clouds rolled up during lunch on that bank holiday Monday, and by the time Harriet was pouring out the coffee, rain was falling and the brightness of spring was blotted out under a leaden sky. The consequent confinement seemed to throw something of a strain on the little party, and Linda took an early opportunity of escaping to the library, delving with eager delight into the rich world it offered. She noticed the slim volume of her father's verse, and took it down. He had signed it. The date was the year before her mother's death, the year of its publication. No more of his verses had been published in book form. The poetry section was sparse and she had moved on to the fiction and was glancing through one of the several books by Henry James when Luke Ferndale came in.

"Harriet said she thought you were in here, my dear. Mustn't hide yourself away, you know."

"What a splendid library! How my father must have envied it!"

"Yes, I think he did. Well now, I want to have a quiet little chat with you, Linda, and we might as well have it here where we'll be undisturbed."

He sat down in a leather armchair and looked at her as she sat, perched on the top of the library steps, a book in her hands.

"Are you comfortable up there?" he asked.

"Yes, thank you."

"Then I'll tell you what I have in mind. I've been thinking about you a lot, my dear. How would you like to go out to Bermuda with my son and his family and take a job in my hotel?"

Linda looked at him in astonished silence for a moment or two, then said:

"I . . . I can't quite grasp it. I know nothing about hotel work."

"That won't matter in this case. It so happens that there will be a vacancy at the information desk of the hotel, where we employ a girl—we call her a hostess—who gives guests any information they want about the island: times of buses, ferries, details about the boating excursions we arrange, any help they need in order to make the most of their holiday. She also arranges tennis fours if wanted, golf pairs or foursomes, hires taxis for the guests, or boats. Whatever guests want, she provides. The hotel has its own tennis courts, golf course and swimming pools, and its own private beach served by the hotel bus. So you see it would be a varied and interesting job, and quite within your scope after a few weeks of studying the island and helping the present hostess until she leaves at the end of May."

"It sounds wonderful, but I've had no experience of dealing with people."

"Exactly. That's why it will be such a valuable experience for you. Teach you to mix. Give you a social education. You have a nice voice and a pleasant manner, when you relax. You'll soon learn, I'm sure. It's a luxury hotel and you'll be dealing with people who know how to behave. I'd like you to have a year there, at least. It will give you the sort of education you need."

Linda flushed, her pride jibbing at his implied criticism although she knew it was fair enough. But would she be suitable for such a job, even after training?

"I've never been abroad," she said simply. "I'd love to see foreign places, of course. But I'm not at all sure that I could do it."

"Nonsense. Only needs intelligence and application. You've got the one and are capable of the other. The polish will come with practice. That's settled, then?"

"But . . . does your son think I'll be suitable?"

"I haven't asked him. If you're agreeable, we'll have him in now and tell him."

"What about clothes, and . . .

He cut her short.

"I shall give you a sum of money sufficient to equip yourself suitably. My daughter-in-law will guide you there. And enough to pay your fare and tide you over until your first month's salary. You'll have no expenses, apart from your appearance, and a little luxury around you will be a pleasant change, I imagine, although you

55

won't allow it to spoil you, I'm sure. You'll have to work quite hard, you know. Always be pleasant and helpful and know your facts."

"It's most generous and kind of you. I feel I ought to regard it as a debt and pay you back some time."

"Nonsense. You are my goddaughter. I look on this as payment for your education. You'll be independent, once you start earning, but the initial outlay will be my gift. I owe that to your mother. Now, what about it, my dear? You won't let this opportunity slip, I'm sure."

If you accept gifts, you lose your independence which is worth more than any gift, her father would say. But don't shrink from life, her instinct said. She gave the old man a smile and said:

"Thank you very much. I'll do my best to make a success of the job."

"Splendid. This is a turning point in your life, Linda, and I'm sure you deserve the opportunity. Now if you'll just go and fetch Austin and his wife, we can get the details settled straight away. Like to get things cut and dried."

She found the whole family gathered

together in the drawing-room, and thought they were arguing, but a sudden silence fell on the room when they saw her. Both Austin and his wife looked surprised at her request, but they went to the library without any questioning. Their reaction to Luke Ferndale's proposal, however, was undisguised astonishment followed by misgivings which they tried to hide once they saw that the old man had made up his mind and was growing testy at Austin's hedging.

"Of course," said Cynthia gaily, trying to paper over the cracks, "we shall enjoy having Linda with us. It's just that it is a tough job for an inexperienced girl. But Sally will be with her to show her the ropes for the first month, and between us we'll get her into shape, no doubt. You do spring things on us though, LG," added Cynthia with arch reproach.

"Keep you on your toes," rejoined Luke. "You must take Linda shopping and equip her with suitable clothes. I'm footing the bill. No need to be sparing, or extravagant. Buy whatever is needed to make her feel well equipped. Sports clothes, too. She'll want to enjoy some tennis and swimming in her spare time."

"We never have any," said Cynthia, laughing.

"Linda will. You must find someone to relieve her so that she has adequate free time. I want her to have a proper education in work and in social life. I know you'll guide her there, Cynthia. I shall come out to see how she's getting on, so do your best."

"Your protégée will be well cared for, I promise you," said Cynthia, putting a friendly hand on Linda's shoulder.

"Thank you, my dear. Now I'll leave you to discuss a programme. There won't be much time. Linda will have to go back to Cornwall for a few days and clear things up there, and you want to be back before the end of the month, so that only gives you about a fortnight. I hope that assistant manager of yours is coping in your absence."

"Ryley's all right, Father," said Austin a little curtly.

"Of course, my boy. You do a good job, you and Cynthia and Roland. A pleasant job, though. Lots of people would envy you, after all. And Linda's going to find it an exciting new life, I'm sure. A very satisfactory Easter, this, from every point of view," concluded Luke Ferndale with the nearest approach to a smile which his severe face could manage. Then he left them.

"Well, you and I will have to put our heads together later on this evening, dear," said Cynthia to Linda. "But just now, I'm helping Angela to work out a list of things we want to buy for the nursery and the baby while we're over here. I'm certainly going to have a wonderful shopping spree."

Austin followed his wife out, leaving Linda a little uncertain about their reaction and in a daze at the way her life had been transformed in the space of half an hour.

6

Consultations

ANGUS was standing in front of the fire rather moodily surveying a glass of sherry when his grandfather came into the room.

"I want a few words with you, my boy. A business matter. Come into my study. We've twenty minutes before dinner."

"Right, sir," said Angus.

In his grandfather's study there was no fire, and the room seemed cold and cheerless.

"Shall I switch on the fire?" asked Angus, as his grandfather sat down.

"Hardly worth it. Shan't keep you long."

"Can I fetch you a drink? I don't like drinking on my own."

"You know I've never approved of this cocktail habit before meals. Ruins your stomach. And sit down, boy. I don't like people looming over me. That's better. Now I'm offering you some business. I want you to investigate the accounts and advise on the tax affairs of the hotel. I'm not satisfied with the present arrangement, and the hotel's not bringing in a proper return on the capital. I'd like a full investigation and report."

"I see." Angus regarded his sherry thoughtfully. "Is Dad in on this?"

"I discussed it with him yesterday. He'd be very glad if you'd take it on. He seemed to think you'd refuse, though. I pointed out that I was only offering myself as a client, not as an employer," said Luke ironically.

"Why me?"

"Because you're a good accountant and my solicitor tells me you are brilliant where tax matters are concerned. I have to accept other people's opinions of my grandson's professional capabilities since he's never put them at my disposal."

Angus eyed his grandfather with a certain wry amusement. This represented a victory, indeed, in their long struggle. For his grandfather to offer himself as a client after washing his hands of him when it became clear that he was not joining the family business was a climbing down unknown in his grandfather's dealings with his family. The old man was frowning, his eyes daring his grandson to register a victory, his jaw thrust forward at its most pugnacious angle.

"Rather an expensive decision, Grandfather. The fare's not exactly a trifle," said Angus wickedly, for Luke's puritan objection to extravagance was growing even stronger with age.

"That's my business, young man. Will you accept the job?"

"They must be in a mess, for you to call me in. Yes, I'll take it on. Never turn away a new client if I can help it."

"H'm. Doing all right since that senior partner of yours retired?"

"You're better informed than I thought. Yes, I prefer it, as a matter of fact. Like you, Grandfather, I like to be the only man on the bridge."

"Heavier responsibility."

"That doesn't worry me. My partner often did. He wanted to coast along at the end. Understandable. But irritating."

"You can be pretty irritating yourself. You're a stubborn, arrogant young man, Angus, but at least you're not woolly-minded. We've not got on well in the past, but you're thirty-one now and I shan't change you. I'll not forgive you for letting a fine business go out of the family, though."

"You got a good price for it. Anyway, Dad was still there, and it was not beyond the bounds of possibility that he would provide some more offspring when he married again."

"You resented that, didn't you?"

"I didn't resent his marrying again, though it was a bit quick, I thought. Sensible of him. I just didn't care for his choice."

"Your stepmother is a charming woman."

"I don't deny it."

"What a damned difficult chap you are, Angus," burst out Luke Ferndale angrily.

"Not at all. I don't interfere in anybody else's lives. They can do what they like. The greatest virtue, Grandfather, is a negative one—not to interfere. But I have my opinions, which I keep to myself—unless pressed," he concluded with a charming smile.

The old man tapped his hand on the arm of his chair. If there was one thing that infuriated him more than another in his dealings with his grandson, it was this silky control which the fellow had over his feelings, so that when at his deadliest, he was at his most polite. It was like dealing with an armadillo: the smooth defence never crumpled. To Luke, who had never found it easy to control his feelings and who often failed, it was unnatural that this young man never lost control. It was not due to any lack of feeling: Angus's passions ran as strongly as his. That, he supposed, was partly the trouble.

"Your father will be glad of your professional help, and glad to see a bit more of you. He's asked you to go out and see the hotel many times and you've always refused, he says."

"I don't find my stepmother's company or Roland's much to my taste. Or luxury hotels, come to that. Of course, going on business will be quite another matter."

"I won't have this division down the family, Angus. It's absurd." But he knew from the ironical lift of his grandson's eyebrows that he was beating air. "What have you against them?" he demanded angrily.

"Let's just say that we're incompatible, shall we?"

"You get your cussedness from your mother. Jane could be very perverse."

"Aunt Harriet maintains that I get it from you. This sherry's a very good one."

"You've heard that I'm sending Linda Dawley out to Bermuda?"

"Yes. Do you think that's wise?"

"Wise? Wise? Of course I do. Why else should I do it?" said Luke testily.

Angus shrugged his shoulders.

"A bit like entering a rowing boat at Cowes, isn't it?"

"I'm looking on it as a finishing school. That girl's had little education and has been living like a primitive peasant looking after a Bohemian father who had no money and no guts. It's not too late, though, to give her a chance of making something of herself. I'm her godfather. I owe it to her mother to do what I can for her. Do you realise that until she came here this weekend, she'd not moved from that isolated spot in Cornwall for the last ten years?"

"Does that fit her for the sophisticated sort of life she'll find at the hotel?"

"It will put a polish on her. It's not as though she won't have guidance. She'll be in the care of your father and Cynthia, and I shall go out there and see how she's getting on."

"Don't show too much interest in her, Grandfather. It might cause jealousy in our happy little family."

"And just what do you mean by that?"

"If you don't know, I'm not telling you."

"It will be a wonderful experience for the girl. Help to give her confidence. She's had a poor enough youth. If you can spare time from your work when you're out there, you might put yourself out now and again to give her what you young people would call a good time. She's earned a little cake."

"I'll lay on a few éclairs, by all means, if I can find the time. She was a nice kid, and still is, no doubt, though I haven't had much time to judge. She's grown a shell, and doesn't find it easy to come out."

"She will. There's a lot of her mother in her, and Diana was a fine woman in every way, as well as an attractive one."

"The age of chivalry lives on in you, Grandfather. The last bastion," said

Angus, laughing, but with an almost affectionate look on his face which was not lost on his grandfather, who said gruffly:

"Must you go back tonight?"

"Yes. This is our busy time of the year. I shan't be able to get out to Bermuda for at least six weeks."

"Very well. I wish you could have stayed here another day. The traffic back will be heavy. It could take you hours to get to London."

"I shan't leave until late. I'll miss it that way."

"Living in a flat in London. Sounds bleak to me. You ought to get married, Angus."

"Not I. That particular cage doesn't appeal to me."

"Cage, nonsense. A home and family give a man a stable background. A good woman can make all the difference to a man's life, my boy."

But when his grandfather started talking about the influence of a good woman, Angus found it time to change the subject. He did so with great cunning.

"I hear that among your many other activities, you're now playing a leading part in local politics. I thought you were agin all political parties."

"So I am. A mixture of charlatanry and imbecility, that's what government is in our time. No respect for the old values. Thrift and virtue despised, the hard-working penalised, the criminals encouraged . . ."

Angus settled back, sipping his sherry, as the explosions rumbled on until the clock struck eight, reminding the old man that one of the virtues which he lived by was punctuality. As Angus followed him to the dining-room, the rumblings still went on, and he marvelled at his grandfather's vigour.

After dinner, Luke, Austin, Cynthia and Roland settled down to bridge, and shortly afterwards Angus saw Linda slip out of the room. Hearing footsteps on the gravel drive outside, he drew the curtains back from the bay window and saw her disappearing round the side of the house. The rain had stopped and it was a fine night with a full moon riding over a group of cypress trees. Angela was sitting by her husband, glancing at his hand and knitting. Harriet was absorbed in a book. Angus decided that the night air was more inviting, and he, too, followed Linda's example.

The air smelt sweet after the rain, and he squared his shoulders and took a deep breath. He found family gatherings oppressive; the presence of his stepmother and step-brother always seemed to put an artificial gloss on the proceedings. He took out his cigarette case. An owl was hooting from the belt of woodland on the far boundary. It was peaceful and quiet enough here. Difficult to think it was a bank holiday. A few miles away, beyond Ellarton, the motorists would be streaming home, unless the rain that afternoon had driven them to return earlier. Funny, the Dawley girl turning up here again. Grandfather had a good memory, and never let go. He fancied he sensed a slight mellowing in the old boy. Musing on the events of the day, wondering how he could fit in the trip to Bermuda, he strolled round the house and across the lawn at the back, then along the path between the herbaceous borders and down the slope to the pool. Linda was sitting on the seat, gazing into the water where the reflection of the moon looked back at her. She had said very little at dinner, but in her shabby tweed dress she had yet taken on an odd, quiet dignity which he had found touching. Before, she had seemed awkward, nervous. This evening, she had still been unable to mix freely, but he felt that she had come to terms with the situation. She looked forlorn now, sitting on the seat, hunched forward, watching the water, oblivious of his presence, for he had come up behind her and the grass had softened his approach.

"Hullo," he said quietly, and she turned, startled. "Can I join you or do you want to be alone?"

"No. I was feeling a little guilty at leaving the party. Now that I'm not the only one, I needn't worry."

"Have you enjoyed the week-end?"

"It's been a great adventure for me. I'd grown so used to my quiet life. It's left me rather breathless, the way my life has taken a completely new turn. I still can't realise that I'm going to Bermuda in two weeks' time. I've never been out of this country, you know. I'm excited and a little afraid that I shan't be any use out there."

"You'll be all right, I expect. Just a question of learning the ropes, as it is with any job. What did you do with yourself in Cornwall?"

"There wasn't much time left after running the cottage and growing our fruit and vegetables, and looking after the chickens. I typed my father's articles and books. And we went on long walks together. Dad was a keen botanist and kept records of all the wild flowers we came across. And when his sight got bad, I read to him. There was never a dull moment, I can tell you."

"I believe you. But then dullness comes from within, doesn't it?"

"Yes. But here, for the first time in my life, I feel I am dull. You're all so . . . different."

"You've just got rusty socially. Why worry? Social gloss isn't important. Comes with practice."

She was silent for a moment, then turned to him.

"Angus, tell me honestly. Do you think I'll be any good at this hotel job? I have a feeling that your father and stepmother aren't in favour, and I'm wondering whether I ought to have accepted if I'm so unfitted for the work. Your grandfather is very kind, but if he's putting a burden on your parents, who run the hotel . . ."

"I've told you. Training and experience will fit you to the job if you want to be fitted. But I'm not altogether in favour of the idea. It's a sophisticated life you're going to. Will you like it?"

"I don't know. But I'd like to try it. And I'd love to see a new country. Your grandfather thinks it will be a splendid education for me, and he's being very generous. I'd hate to disappoint him. But I'm twenty-four. Isn't that a bit late to change? I have an idea your parents aren't optimistic."

Angus knocked the ash off his cigarette and was silent. How explain to this girl the undercurrents in the family? The warfare that went on all the time.

"Please don't think I'm criticising your father or stepmother," she went on, misreading his silence. "They've been most kind. Your stepmother, particularly, is going out of her way to reassure me. But if I'm obviously a hopeless candidate, it is a bit tiresome for them to have me foisted on them."

Again he hesitated, then decided against giving any warning at this stage.

"You're taking it all too seriously," he said. "Grandfather thinks you've had a lean time and he's anxious to give you a treat. Whether you fit the job or not, he wants you to enjoy yourself and see how the rest of the world lives. He can well afford it, and as his godchild and the daughter of a very close friend, you need feel no qualms about letting him indulge you and himself. Believe me, he doesn't do much indulging. Having accepted his offer, relax, and make the most of it."

"Thank you. That's relieved my mind. Do you know Bermuda?"

"I spent two days there on my way back from New York some years ago. I'm coming out there shortly on business, though, and Grandfather has suggested that I might give you a few leads on how to enjoy yourself, that is if you haven't already discovered that for yourself."

"Your grandfather's not as alarming as I once thought."

"Alarming? Well, in a rage, he could be alarming to the uninitiated. He has an old-fashioned desire always to spare the ladies, though, so you probably won't ever see him in full spate. He's an amazing character. Stubborn, self-willed, a ruthless dictator. Yet he can be generous and chivalrous. A puritanical upholder of moral virtues, with all the intolerance of the upright. We've had a very stormy relationship since I opted for independence, but I fancy he's coming round a bit in his old age. Have to watch him, though. He's a past master at giving an inch, then gaining a yard while you're off balance."

"A state you're seldom in, I'm sure," said Linda gravely.

"Can't afford to be in this wicked world, my girl. That's something I've learned."

"You learned it at a very tender age, then, because you were always certain of your balance when I knew you, and that's going back to your schooldays. Often I was content to trot round obediently, but sometimes I jibbed. You were just as much a dictator as your grandfather ever was."

"Never. I respect other people's right to run their own lives. You were a kid and had to be looked after."

"And that eventually became a bore."

"Shall we say that other diversions took up my time?"

"And they were all so attractive."

"Well, we all go through the soft-boiled egg stage."

"What a depressing way of putting it. Are you so hard-boiled now?"

"Hard as stone."

"Are you the right person to show me how to enjoy myself, then?" she asked, laughing.

"Of course. Enjoyment without any painful sequel. It's the romantic types that do the damage."

"I wouldn't know. But I think you'd be an odd person if you never lost your heart."

"That goes for a woman, perhaps. Men have other spheres to absorb them."

"I shall enjoy reminding you of that lofty statement one day. I hope I'm around when you fall."

"I'm beginning to recognise Lindey Lou."

"When will you be coming out to Bermuda?"

"Might manage it about the end of May. You'll like it there. Lovely climate, coral beaches, and a paradise for flower-lovers. I haven't seen the Caythorpe Hotel. It's the other end of the island from where I stayed. But it's very plushy. Can't imagine a greater contrast to a cottage in Cornwall. Hope you've got a steady head."

"Steady as a rock," she assured him gravely, with that little note of laughter in her voice which he had heard before.

"I'm not suggesting that you're a feather-brained child, but you're very inexperienced to be thrown into a sophisticated life. Don't take everything at face value. People are not always what they seem."

"I'll remember," she said gravely, and he shot a quick glance at her, but she kept a poker face.

"Well, we'd better show ourselves back at the house, or they'll be sending a search-party," he said.

They walked back through the moonlit garden, talking of Bermuda and all it promised, until Linda stopped in the shadow of a beech tree.

"Look, Angus. There's a hedgehog. I had a tame one at the cottage. Of course we called her Mrs. Tiggy-Winkle. They're poppets, aren't they? So slow and deliberate and absorbed."

The hedgehog made its ponderous journey across the lawn and disappeared under the hedge, where they heard it snuffling and rustling in the dead leaves. Angus took Linda's arm as they went on, somewhat reluctantly, towards the house.

In the hall, Cynthia, elegant in a grey lace suit with a diamond spray winking in the lapel, was showing Angela some pieces of china from a corner cabinet. Angela, in a black silk dress, had a piece of Crown Derby in her hand as they turned at the sound of the door.

"Ah, here are our truants," said Cynthia with a dazzling smile.

Angus eyed them calmly: Angela, whose fair colouring showed up to great advantage against the pretty black dress, and Cynthia, smooth and polished like the diamonds she wore. He supposed it would be difficult to find two more decorative women under one roof. Their synthetic charm appealed to him as little as artificial flowers. He preferred the girl in the shabby green dress who liked hedgehogs and read Beatrix Potter.

7

Cold water

ON her last day at Hartfield, Linda was cutting the grass paths in the vegetable garden while Amos was threading black cotton patiently among the runner beans which were just coming through.

"Them devils of pigeons will have all the shoots off 'em if I don't watch out," he said, as Linda finished the last path and stood by the mower, watching him.

"Just think, Amos. This time tomorrow I shall have flown more than three thousand miles across the Atlantic and be on an island of coral beaches, where there are hedges of hibiscus and morning glory, and the sun always shines."

"Fancy," said Amos without any great show of enthusiasm.

"Imagine what wonderful plants you could grow in that climate. Bananas and date palms, bougainvillaea, oleanders."

78

"I've enough to do coping with British plants. And wherever you are, there's always enemies to contend with. Nature's the same, all the world over."

"But imagine never having any cold weather."

"Hurricanes and storms instead, I dare say."

"Oh, Amos, what a pessimist you are!"

"Not a pessimist, Lindey. Just not taken in by them tourist adverts. This country's good enough for me. Don't know why everybody has to keep tearing about these days. Never get to know any place properly, not even the place where they live. And if you can't think of anything better to do than moon there talking, I can."

"Well, I've finished the grass. What else can I do?"

"Finished the grass? What about them edges? Look right slovenly, they do. Like a man who hasn't shaved for a week. The edging shears are in the shed. If you do a job for me, it has to be done properly."

Meekly, Linda went to the shed to fetch the shears. Amos was in one of his less mellow moods, due, she suspected, to the fact that the finches had pecked most of the buds from his favourite flowering cherry tree and left them scattered on the grass below for his eyes to fall on that morning.

Nor was Harriet, who was picking some daffodils in the orchard, any more enthusiastic when Linda joined her there after finishing the edges.

"I'm too excited to think straight today," said Linda, "but I can probably manage to cut off the dead heads to Amos's liking."

"Have you finished your packing?" asked Harriet.

"As far as I can. I've never had so many clothes to pack in my life before. I still feel that I'm in a dream. You've travelled a lot, I expect, Miss Ferndale."

"When I was younger. I usually went with my father on his business trips. A sort of stand-in secretary."

"Where did you go?"

"Oh, Europe, America, the Bahamas."

"Sounds wonderful."

"It was interesting, but the actual travelling was tedious. Aeroplanes must be the most boring way of travel ever devised."

To Linda, who saw aeroplanes as magic carpets, this was hard to accept. She tried again.

"Which was your favourite place?"

"Oh, I don't know. France, I think. I wasn't sorry when Father retired and business travelling stopped. I'd grown out of it. All cities are the same now—noisy, full of traffic, with great blocks of ugly modern hotels. I've no wish to go abroad again."

"Well, I've never been out of this country, so the lure of the unknown works for me. But you and Amos are certainly trying to keep my feet on the ground," said Linda, smiling, and wishing she could break the reserve of this odd woman with the thin face and rather striking dark eyes.

"You take yourself with you, wherever you go," said Harriet briefly.

"Yes, that's true. The one thing we can't escape from—ourselves. My father often said that."

"Was he happy, your father, after he escaped from us?"

"Yes, I think he was. During the last few years, anyway, he gained a certain peace of mind. He accepted his failure then, and with nobody to remind him of it, it didn't seem to matter so much."

"Poor Stuart. He had a small talent. Not

nearly bright or bold enough to shine in our sort of world. He was too sensitive a plant altogether. It's to be hoped you've inherited some of your mother's resilience. Father was asking for you. An old friend of his has arrived and will be staying for this farewell dinner tonight. You'd better come in and meet him."

Linda followed her back to the house, thinking what an austere, difficult person she was to know. On the terrace, she met Luke Ferndale with a tall, thin, white-haired man.

"Ah, there you are, my dear. Come and be introduced to a very dear old friend of mine, Mr. Brookwood. This is my god-daughter, Linda Dawley."

Mr. Brookwood took her hand with a kind smile that was reassuring.

"You can imagine, John, how good it is to have her back in the fold again, after losing touch for ten years," went on Luke.

"Yes, indeed. But you're sending her away so soon."

"Only to further her education, and I shall be going out to Bermuda myself to see that all's well with her. She'll be in good hands with Cynthia and Austin."

But I'm twenty-four, and I've looked after a home and a father for years, protested Linda silently. You speak as though I'm a child you've adopted from an orphanage. But his kindness and generosity to her kept her from speaking her thoughts. In the past two weeks, he had spared no effort to make her feel that she mattered to him, and that in future she need have no cares which he would not shift from her shoulders. She was grateful, but felt a little smothered, and looked forward to seeing Angus again that evening. She had not seen him since the Easter week-end, and she felt in need of his bracing presence in spite of the fact that he, too, had treated her as though she was no more mature now than she had been at fourteen. Now, as then, his careless assumption of authority pricked her, but at twenty-four she could smile at it, whereas at fourteen she had often been enraged by it.

He arrived just before dinner, and they were joined, too, by a middle-aged man with an ugly but pleasant face and a breezy manner; his name was Philip Hanwood and he was the headmaster of the local preparatory school. Linda learned that he had just returned from a holiday in Greece.

It was a lively dinner party, with everybody in good form. Linda, still inhibited on social occasions, was glad to have old Mr. Brookwood as her neighbour. She learned that he was a botanist and was able to tell him of her father's interest in plants. She knew so little of the subjects the others discussed: Greece, the economy of Bermuda, the well-known people who had stayed at the hotel and about whom she was woefully ignorant, in spite of Cynthia's efforts to jog her memory.

"But you must have read some newspapers when you were in Cornwall, surely," said Cynthia, smiling incredulously.

"Very seldom. My father held the view that what was in them was either rubbish or inaccurate, and he refused to tire his eyes with newsprint. I relied on the radio."

"My dear, you *have* got a lot to learn," said Cynthia.

"How extraordinary!" said Angela. "No newspapers."

"Your father was very wise," said John Brookwood in his quiet, deliberate voice.

"A sheer waste of time, nine-tenths of the contents of newspapers. And you get to an age when you decide you haven't that amount of time to waste."

"But you must keep in touch with the life of the nation," said Roland.

"When you've read the newspaper, how much of it do you remember two hours later?" asked Harriet sharply.

"Well, I mean to say . . ." Roland stumbled, then recovered himself. "Well, you just ought to know what's going on."

Harriet fixed him with her dark eyes.

"Why? Do you mean to do anything about it? Mr. Brookwood is right. Nine-tenths of a newspaper isn't news, it's opinion and gossip. Anything that matters can be heard on the radio. Personally, I think we'd all be better with a lot less news. Far too much rammed down our throats."

"Hear, hear!" said Angus. "Less news and less government, that's what we want."

"I think you're all talking a lot of nonsense," said Cynthia gaily.

To Linda's relief, Angus and Philip Hanwood began an argument about a recent biography, in which Harriet joined, and she hoped she would not be the focus of attention again, but Luke Ferndale brought her back into the spotlight by proposing a toast which she found highly embarrassing.

"Let's drink to my goddaughter's venture into the world. Her first trip abroad; may it teach her a lot and give the enjoyment she's never had and richly deserves."

They lifted their glasses, and Linda felt herself blushing as she murmured her thanks.

"But this is your home, my dear," went on Luke. "Don't forget that. If you're not happy out there, you can come back any time. In any case, after a year I shall want you back. I haven't found you again just to lose you to Bermuda."

"I . . . I don't know what to say. You've all been so kind to me."

"Poor Linda," said Cynthia. "It must be a little overwhelming to be adopted by a family so quickly."

"That's not right, Cynthia," said Luke. "Linda always was part of our family until her mother died and her father took her away. That was just an interruption. She always belonged to Hartfield."

"Lucky Linda," said Cynthia. "It's a

very nice family to belong to, and I should know."

Linda saw Angus, opposite her, roll up his eyes, and Harriet said briskly:

"Have you managed to buy that extra ground for another playing-field, Philip?"

The moment passed and the conversation became general again, but Linda had sensed a tension in the air which she could not explain. As the talk went on around her, she had a strange sensation of being trapped. How had it come about? She had come here on a visit. Now, after only two weeks, she was part of the Ferndale family, off to Bermuda under Mr. Ferndale's auspices, there to be educated and returned to him at Hartfield. Happy and excited as she was at the prospect of seeing another country, of earning good money at an interesting job, she had not realised until that moment just how completely old Mr. Ferndale had annexed her. Give him an inch and he'll take a yard, Angus had said. She was learning the truth of that. And yet, could one protest at kindness?

To her disappointment, she had little contact with Angus that evening. Only when she was about to go to bed did he stop her at the foot of the stairs to wish her a pleasant journey to Bermuda.

"You're not coming to the airport with your grandfather to see us off, then?"

"No. I'm leaving before breakfast in the morning. Have to be back at the office."

"And you'll be coming out when?"

"Not quite certain yet. Probably at the beginning of June. Enjoy yourself."

He gave her a brief smile and turned as Harriet came into the hall with Jason, the lugubrious old mastiff.

"Going out?" asked Angus, as his aunt made for the vestibule.

"Just taking Jason for his evening constitutional."

"I'll join you, if you've no objection."

He helped his aunt into her tweed coat which always hung in the vestibule, and they went out together. Linda, feeling rather blank, walked slowly up the stairs. The others had all gone to bed. She had lingered, hoping to have a few words alone with Angus. She felt in need of the assurance he gave her, and she decided to get up early and see him before he left.

With her packing completed, she checked again the contents of her handbag to make sure that her passport and other necessities were there, and prepared for bed. She was tired, and within a very short space of time she was lying in bed, watching the moon through the open window, still scarcely able to believe that she would be flying across the Atlantic the next day.

She was beginning to float away in the arms of sleep when footsteps on the terrace below brought her back. She heard the sound of a match being struck, then Angus's voice.

"Grand view from the terrace here, especially by moonlight."

"A pity you don't come more often to see it, my boy."

"Well, you know how things are with the old man and me. We go up in flames. That last row we had was the row to end all rows."

"He misses you. It's been a little better this time, though, hasn't it?"

"Yes. He's at last accepted the fact that I'm independent and intend to remain so. But the family doesn't get any easier to stomach with the years. I'm beginning to regret having agreed to go out to Bermuda.

My investigations won't be exactly popular, and I loathe getting involved with them."

"Why did you agree, then?"

"Must have been bowled over by the fact that Grandfather actually asked me to accept him as a client."

"Don't sound so gloomy. It's a pleasant place to go to, and you'll probably enjoy it well enough."

"I never enjoy being in the company of my stepmother and her son. And I've promised to give Linda a bit of fun. I must have been doped when I agreed to get involved like this."

"Linda's a nice enough girl. That shouldn't be too onerous a duty."

"Wide-eyed innocents up from the country aren't my line. And wouldn't you think Grandpa would have more sense than to plug her like this in front of my stepmother? For all his shrewdness, in some ways the old man's an absolute babe. As blind as a bat where women are concerned."

"Where *pretty* women are concerned. He believes no nasty thought can live inside a pretty feminine head."

"It's pathetic, isn't it? And he's so

pleased with himself, sending his Cinderella to the ball. Well, there's nothing I can
do about it, and I'd have been wiser to have
kept out of it altogether."

"Cheer up. Linda may find a rich
husband at the hotel and take herself
off."

"I doubt it. The competition's fierce."

"That's a somewhat cynical observation."

"I'm not in my sunniest mood. The
realisation of what I've let myself in for
grows."

"Well, why not take the optimistic view?
A job of work in a pleasant place. And
giving a young woman who's not had much
fun a few days' enjoyment. You're very
good at that, I'm sure."

"If you take a girl out to tea in Cornwall,
you're probably as good as betrothed. Go
to a dance together, and you've as good as
signed the mortgage and chosen a cottage
near a school. Before I know where I am,
I'll be up to my neck in a morass of tears
and reproaches."

By this time, Linda had shaken off the
drowsy inertia of the threshold to sleep,
and she slipped out of bed and went quickly

to the window, closing it quietly. They were leaning on the terrace below, the dog flopped down behind them. She could see the glowing ends of their cigarettes.

Back in bed, she simmered at Angus's arrogance as she had often simmered in the past. She was wrong in thinking he could no longer make her angry. Then her sense of the absurd came to her rescue. What he had said, although wounding to her pride, was logical enough, and pride was a foolish thing. She would bear it in mind when he came out to Bermuda, though, and she would certainly not rise early to see him the next morning. With which conclusion, she fell into a deep sleep.

Had she heard the rest of their conversation, however, she might have been more troubled.

"Well, I can't help feeling sorry for that girl," Harriet said, "and I can't imagine what will come out of this situation Father's made. In some ways, he's so insensitive, you can't believe it. He insisted on my giving Linda the guest suite with her own bathroom, when your parents always have it when they stay here. They've had to go in the turret room and share our bathroom.

And Cynthia spends hours in the bathroom. I can't imagine what she does there. Only a small thing, Father would say, but to a woman like your stepmother, a snub. And on the grounds of numbers alone, it would have been more suitable to give the larger room and private bathroom to two people instead of one. But Father has absolutely no tact. No sensibility."

"He never sees the other person's point of view. Just blindly determined that everything shall be as he wants it. This whole business presents such a gratifying picture to him. His goddaughter, rescued from poverty and given the sort of opportunity every girl dreams of, with some work thrown in to meet his puritan belief that all play and no work is corrupting. She'll come back a social asset, groomed by Cynthia, of all people, and be grateful to him for the rest of his days, and console him in his old age. That's how he sees it."

"Well, I suppose it could be like that."

"Do you really think Cynthia will play the part he's allotted her? She and Roland are both mad that Grandfather hasn't done anything about his will. She'll see Linda as a usurper."

"Well, what can she do about it? History is against her."

"I don't know. But to send a totally inexperienced girl out to a luxury hotel, to transport her from a simple rural existence of near poverty to a sophisticated, wealthy environment under the guidance of a woman who resents her, is asking for trouble."

"Aren't you seeing Linda as a helpless child, when she is in fact a young woman of twenty-four who isn't without experience of responsibility? I know she seems unarmed, but that's because solitude hasn't provided her with any social finish. But what does that amount to? A set of pretty tricks of behaviour. I've a feeling she's got a steadier head than you think."

"I hope you're right. I've only seen her on two occasions since she came back, and then only briefly. You've seen more of her. I can't help feeling uneasy, that's all."

"And annoyed because you don't really want to be involved, but you are?"

"Clever Aunt Harriet. You read me like a book . . . almost."

"Well, don't lose any sleep over it."

"I shan't. But Grandfather and trouble are synonymous, and I'm willing to bet that this latest happy project will prove no exception."

8

The Caythorpe Hotel

THE main hall of the Caythorpe Hotel was always the scene of much activity and Linda surveyed it from behind her desk on that warm day at the end of May with just as much amazement and interest as she had felt on her first day. Her preconceived notion of the hotel had proved completely wrong. She had visualised it as the kind of Grand Hotel of the English seaside holiday resort. What she had found had been a completely self-contained colony within the boundaries of the hotel and its grounds. A colony given over to sport, amusement and superb comfort, so that guests had no need to step beyond the Caythorpe boundaries; everything they could want to buy or do was available there.

The hall itself, with its central massed bank of plants and flowers, its lavish carpet and chandelier, was the hub of the place, for radiating from it were the main lounge and dining-room, and the long dining terrace. Some golfers walked across just then, discussing their game, and a party of women in Bermuda shorts and large sun-hats came in from the courtyard and its swimming pools. Four tennis players flopped on one of the enormous sofas that lined the perimeter, and groups of newcomers stood around, suitcases beside them, waiting for the porter, for an aeroplane had recently arrived from New York. And everywhere, the sound of American voices.

It was her first day on duty without Sally, who had flown back to her home in America on the previous day. Meanwhile, another assistant had been trained with her so that between them they could be on duty fourteen hours a day. Jean, a cheerful young Canadian, was due to take over in a few minutes, and Linda was reflecting with a certain satisfaction that her first morning in charge had passed off satisfactorily when Cynthia came up.

"Everything all right, Linda?"

"Yes, thank you, Mrs. Ferndale."

"Good. Mr. Ferndale won't be able to

get away to meet Angus, after all. Would you go to the airport instead? I've told Rollo to hire a taxi. It will be here at two-thirty. By the time Angus arrives, his father will be free."

Cynthia smiled and went. Although she had been as pleasant to Linda as before, there was a subtle difference in her attitude now from that shown to her at Hartfield. Here, there was an unmistakable ring of authority, and it had become obvious to Linda that Mrs. Ferndale took a greater part in managing the hotel than she had suggested, and that beneath the feminine charm lay a businesslike capability.

Delighted at the prospect of seeing Angus again in spite of her determination to play it cool with that autocratic young man, she handed over to Jean a few minutes later and hurried down a flight of stairs leading from the lower hall to the shopping arcade, where a coffee shop sold snacks. Perched on a stool, she watched the deft coloured waitress behind the bar prepare a toasted sandwich and the green salad which was automatically served with it. With an iced fresh orange drink, it made a pleasant meal, for in this warm climate she preferred a light diet.

So much had been crammed into the past few weeks that already it seemed a lifetime since she left London, and everything that had gone before seemed dim and unreal, except Angus, who never in any circumstances would seem dim. Back in her room, she slipped into a coral-coloured sleeveless frock and wondered whether he would see any difference in her, for she felt a different person. She put on a wide-brimmed straw hat, her skin having not yet fully acclimatised itself to the strength of the sun, and ran along the corridor to the lift.

The aeroplane touched down on time, and when Angus came into the airport lounge and looked round, his eyes skated over her, unrecognising, looking for his father. In a grey lounge suit, a raincoat over his arm and carrying a brief-case, he looked very businesslike in this land of sunshine holidays. Then he saw her and smiled.

"Hullo, Angus. It's good to see you. I'm deputising for your father. He was detained."

"Hullo. You look as though the luxury life suits you. All well?"

"Fine. The taxi's waiting. Did you have a good flight?"

"Very smooth."

"The jets are wonderful, aren't they? I simply couldn't believe we were travelling at more than five hundred miles an hour. Whenever I looked out at that blue vault, we seemed to be standing still."

As the taxi moved off on its journey through winding lanes between hedges of hibiscus, he leaned back, stretching his legs.

"You look tired, Angus."

"Life's been a bit hectic. Difficult to leave a practice for any length of time. But I was able to get a report finished on the journey, so I can forget the office for a bit and concentrate on this set-up. What's it like at the hotel?"

"I can only think of one adjective: fabulous."

"I can imagine," he said, with a faint grin. "And the island?"

"I haven't had much opportunity to explore outside the hotel grounds yet, but they extend for miles and take in a beach, and nothing that I've seen outside compares with it. The hotel golf course runs along by the sea and goes up hill and down dale, so that golfers use little motor-carts to get about."

"Not my game, golf."

"The swimming is heavenly; the sea's beautifully warm, and we have heated and unheated pools in the hotel courtyards, surrounded by palm trees and exotic gardens."

"And less decorative females sunbathing, I guess."

"Well, perhaps I can tempt you with our two hard tennis courts, or our boats. You can hire masks and fins, take water-skiing lessons, or be thoroughly old-fashioned and hire a bicycle."

"Tell me more," murmured Angus. "The hotel I stayed at when I was here was a little homelier."

"The Caythorpe has its own night club, with floor shows most evenings. In the lounge next to the dining-room there is always music of one kind or another: old-fashioned songs and piano music alternating with native bands. We cater for all tastes. Social activities are posted daily on the board by my reception desk."

"You must be kept busy."

"I am. There are two of us, working on a rota system."

"Some change from looking after the chickens and growing potatoes in Cornwall," said Angus, smiling.

"I did do other things in Cornwall, too, you know."

"Does that all seem impossibly remote and primitive now?"

"Remote, yes. Primitive? In many ways, far more civilised than life at the Caythorpe."

He looked at her then, as though seeing her for the first time.

"You're not as young as I thought, Linda."

"Young being a polite word for callow?"

"Wow. You've learned to box."

"Not fair, when you're tired. I hope you'll be able to make this a bit of a holiday as well as a job of work. And that *doesn't* mean I include myself in the holiday. You look as though you could do with a rest."

"When your sex gets solicitous, it's time to take wing," he said, his eyes teasing her. "What other delights can you offer me at the Caythorpe?"

"Some people are hard to please. We

have reclining chairs by a waterfall, pool and beach bars, shops, including a barber's, and a valet service. We introduce you to tennis players, golfers, and we even have a host in the dining-room to introduce you to congenial companions to share your table if you do not like your own company."

"Ghastly," said Angus.

"Americans are friendlier than the English."

"More talkative. What about beautiful girls? Aren't they laid on, too?"

"They are all around you," said Linda gravely, and he laughed.

"Well, I can see you've learned your stuff as hostess. Congratulations on being so adaptable."

"Well, to be honest, I feel it's not me here at all. I'm just acting a part. But I'm enjoying it."

"I'm glad. Must say it has its ironical aspect; my puritan grandfather who believes in hard work, thrift and plain living, owning a hotel like this. Of course, he's only concerned with it as a business, and the customers must be given what they want if it's to pay. But a night club, native bands, and Luke Ferndale have a certain comic incongruity that appeals to me."

"Nevertheless, we have certain standards of decorum which your grandfather would approve of. Short shorts and bikinis are not permitted in the public rooms, covering coats are required over swimsuits when going to and from the pools or beach, and most gentlemen wear evening dress for dinner, and everybody does on Thursday and Saturday evenings."

"Well, well. So the old colonial standards linger on still. You've painted quite an enticing picture. As good as a holiday brochure."

"But I haven't mentioned the heavenly sunshine, which is never oppressive, and the blue blue sea, and the gorgeous flowers."

"There *must* be some drawbacks."

"There's not much solitude, and there are no country walks. A lot of the beaches are privately owned, and although the lanes are pretty, there's a fair amount of traffic on them."

"Plenty of fun and games, and no contemplation."

"You could put it like that."

"You appear to have kept your head admirably, Linda."

"Thank you."

"It's early days yet, of course."

"Yes," she said demurely. "If you decide to give me a little fun, I can't answer for the consequences, of course. This," she added hastily as she saw the expression on his face, "is the drive to the hotel."

"I couldn't very well miss that sign. I sense a slight needling in your attitude, my girl, that I'll return to at a more convenient time. Must say there's something romantic about palm trees waving against a blue sky, even to a hard-boiled realist like me," he added as the taxi drove up an avenue of royal palms and finally swung round an island ablaze with bougainvillaea to draw up in front of the high white cliff of the Caythorpe Hotel, in the palm-shaded portico of which stood the beaming coloured major-domo resplendent in his red and blue uniform with shining brass buttons, white gloves and top hat.

"Eureka!" said Angus.

9

On the job

LINDA saw little of Angus during his first week at the hotel, for she was only free in the afternoons, when he was working. At the end of the week, however, he came up to the desk to find out what free time she would have the following week.

"Evenings, from six," she said, and broke off to smile at an American couple and tell them that she had found a Mr. and Mrs. Greenslade who would be delighted to make up a four at tennis.

"Wull, that's fine," said the man. "You did tell them that we're not exactly Forest Hills class?"

"Nor are they. I'm sure you'll enjoy playing with them. They were here a few moments ago. Yes, there they are, over by the bulletin board. Let me introduce you."

Linda shepherded her charges over to the Greenslades and stayed chatting with them for a few moments. When she came back, Angus eyed her with a respectful grin, but before he could say anything, a woman in bright green Bermuda shorts and a pink shirt said:

"Do you have a bus time-table, honey? It's a bit expensive using taxis every-where."

"Yes, of course. Here it is. What route were you wanting? Can I help you?"

"No, thanks. We'll just study it at our leisure. My husband just loves time-tables. Much obliged."

"You're welcome," said Linda, smiling.

"That I should live to see the day!" said Angus, when they were alone. "Smooth as any PRO. And here comes another customer."

"If you could come back in ten minutes. I'll be off duty."

"Not I. I'll wait. I wouldn't miss this performance for the world," he said wick-edly, propping himself up on the counter and leafing through a pamphlet describing places of interest in Bermuda. Linda gave him a cool look and turned her attention to the man who wanted to make reservations for his family on the next day's boat cruise.

After that, it was the turn of a small girl, wearing what Linda had learned were called pedal-pushers of faded blue with a red cotton shirt. She had a round, earnest, little face and wore her hair in a bobbing pony-tail.

"What time is the next bus to the beach, please?" she asked.

"Not until two-thirty now. You've just missed the last morning bus, I'm afraid."

"Too bad," said a dark, sallow-skinned man, looming up. "What do you say to hiring one of those motor-bicycles and I'll take you on the back, Midge?"

Midge smiled her approval, revealing a gap in her front teeth.

"Can we get anything to eat at the beach?" asked the man.

"Yes. Snacks and drinks are available at the beach hut," said Linda. "Can you swim, Midge?"

"Daddy's teaching me. I can nearly."

"She sure is a tryer," said her father, putting his arm round the child's thin shoulders. "Thanks a lot."

"You're welcome," said Linda, smiling, and turned to deal with a woman who wanted to know where she could buy tennis balls.

"At the golf club-house. And you can hire rackets there, too. You may like details of the tennis tournament we're running next week," said Linda, handing her a notice.

"Thanks, honey. Not that Sam and I are much good. Still, that doesn't matter as long as we all enjoy ourselves, does it?"

"That's our wish. You'll find it's a very free and easy affair."

"Much obliged."

"You're welcome," said Linda, smiling, and wished that she could hit Angus over the head, for his evident enjoyment of her performance was galling.

She was kept fully occupied until Jean turned up to relieve her. Emerging from behind her counter, Linda eyed Angus's wicked face with some severity.

"Well, well. Does it go on like that all the time?" he asked.

"It slackens off a little mid-morning and mid-afternoon, and it's definitely quieter in the evenings, but we don't get much time to dream."

"I'll say. Come and have lunch with me."

"Thanks."

"Coffee shop or dining terrace?"

"Coffee shop, please. I don't like a big meal at midday."

"Nor me."

They found a small table in a corner and gave their order for toasted sandwiches and salad.

"Didn't realise this place was so Americanised. Do you have any English people at the hotel?" asked Angus.

"Very few."

"How do you like the Americans?"

"Very much. They're so friendly and uninhibited. It makes my job a pleasure."

"No difficult customers?"

"Not so far."

"Well, I'd be screaming by the end of the day if I were you. But then, I haven't your pleasant, helpful nature."

"It's interesting. All types of people. Hullo, Peter," she added as a tall, sandy-haired man left his seat at the counter and hovered at their table.

"Sorry to butt in, but I wanted to give you this for your collection, Linda. It's called St. Andrew's Cross. Found it yesterday in Paget. It's fairly common there."

"Thank you very much. You're a great help. I don't seem to have had much time yet to go plant-hunting."

He turned to Angus.

"Will you be wanting me this afternoon, Mr. Ferndale? Because if not, your father wants me to go to the bank in Hamilton for him."

"No, I shan't be wanting you, Holmfield, thanks. If I've any queries, they can wait."

"Right."

He went out and Angus looked at the flower beside Linda's plate.

"What's that in aid of? Didn't know he was a botanist. Or you."

"I've always been interested in wild flowers, and I promised your grandfather's friend, Mr. Brookwood, that I'd make a collection and keep records of the wild flowers here so that he can compare them with the flora of the West Indies, which he knows. He's a botanist and is interested in seeing what difference this slightly more temperate climate makes. Peter Holmfield happened to see my record book one day, and told me he was interested in wild flowers and would let me have any he found."

"Nice change from book-keeping," said Angus.

"Yes. Is he a good book-keeper?"

"Very."

"Do you find it dull? Book-keeping. After all, that's part of your job, isn't it?"

"Not exactly. We come in at the next stage. Deal with what the books tell us. My practice is mainly a tax practice, anyway. Most of my work is as a tax consultant. I don't find that dull. And figures have their own fascination, you know. There's a satisfaction in reducing chaos to order, in getting the picture clear. But I'm not going to talk shop. You say you're free in the evenings next week. What about relaxing from our work and having that fun we promised ourselves?"

"You'd really like that?"

"I shouldn't suggest it if I didn't. Why the doubt?"

"Well, you were told to do it, as a sort of duty, weren't you? I've a feeling that you would prefer not to be involved with a wide-eyed innocent."

He looked at her through narrowed eyes.

"Come on. Come clean. What gave you that idea?"

"Well, you," she said delicately, and told him when.

He laughed and said:

"Fair cop. I'd had a particularly trying day that day and wasn't feeling at my best. Perhaps it's as well that you heard, though. I wouldn't want you to get the wrong impression, Linda. That could be hurtful. Enjoyment only. No more."

She looked at him, head on one side like an enquiring robin, her brown eyes dancing, and said:

"I promise I won't lose my heart."

"You think I'm conceited?"

"No. But you think I'm a child."

"A child with some disconcerting tricks, then. Damn it all, I'm just trying to be honest."

"You don't have to try. You are honest, Angus. Believe me, you don't have to spell it out. It's quite understandable that you should think I'd led such a simple quiet life that I'd leap to wrong conclusions at the first attentions from a personable young man. There were *some* males in Cornwall, you know."

"What a gentle manner to go with the scalpel," said Angus, putting his head between his hands. "I give up."

"But not many males," she added wickedly, "and none as attractive as you."

"Lindey Lou, I cry for mercy. No wonder I fled to other more comfortable companions when we were young. Stop needling me and tell me whether you fancy the Gala dinner and dance in the club-room on Monday evening."

"I fancy it very much."

"Right. I'll reserve a table, then. Did I spot you going to the swimming pool early this morning? From the top floor balcony, I couldn't be sure. Black and white swim-suit."

"Yes. I always go in before breakfast. It's empty then."

"Good idea. I'll join you. At any other time of the day, with all those sun-worshippers lying on their chair-beds round the pool, just watching, I'd feel like

114

a goldfish in a bowl. Does anybody actually go in swimming? You're the only person I've seen in that water."

"A few go in. Mostly men and children. But lying round the perimeter is more popular, and some of those gorgeous swim-suits would be ruined by water."

"We live and learn. You looked to be rather a good swimmer, with a nice line in diving. Do a lot in Cornwall?"

"Yes. There was one sandy cove I could reach by bicycle where the bathing was good. It's a dangerous coast, though, and that was the only safe spot within reach."

"Wish I could take a few hours off this afternoon, but I'd better press on. It's a tougher job than I expected. How long are you off duty?"

"Until six this evening."

"How about meeting me here for tea at quarter to five, and coming for a stroll after?"

"I'd like that."

"Have you made any friends here, Linda? Do you get on well with the rest of the staff?"

"Very well. I've made one friend. Ruth Elsted, your father's secretary."

"Yes, I quite take to what I've seen of her. Quiet, but charming in an unobtrusive way. Looks rather fragile."

"She is, I think, but she never talks about her health. She was very kind to me the first week or two, when I was a bit out of my element. She has a ramshackle old car she takes me around in. When our free time coincides, we often spend it together."

"And the family? How are they looking after you? Do you find them helpful?"

"I see hardly anything of your father. He's behind the scenes. Your mother . . ."

"My stepmother," he corrected her quickly.

"She's very charming, and efficient, too. Roland I don't take to, and I hardly see Angela. They live in that pretty bungalow down the lane behind the golf club-house, but I haven't been invited there yet."

"What exactly does Roland do? I've been told that he's sports manager, but I haven't seen him in action."

"He spends most of his time at the golf club-house, I think. He's been very friendly to me. I've no complaint. I just don't know the man behind the smiling surface. And he's a gossip. A good mixer, though, and I should think very useful here."

"You haven't many kindred souls around you, then."

"I've only been here six weeks. Peter Holmfield is a dear, and he has a delightful boy, David. He's ten and goes to school in Hamilton. Peter's wife, Enid, is one of the housekeepers. She manages the maids and is responsible for the top floor rooms."

"The Holmfields live in the staff quarters on the other side of the golf course, I suppose?"

"Yes."

"And where are you?"

"I'm tucked away in a little room on the top floor of the hotel. Too small for guests, but it has a balcony and a grand view. I'm very happy there."

"It's worked out all right, then. I'm glad. Have you heard from the old man?"

"I had a letter last week. He wants me to keep in touch."

"You'd better. Now I must return to my figures, unless you'd like more coffee?"

"No, thank you. I'm going down to the beach for a swim this afternoon."

"Lucky you. Until quarter to five, then."

10

Waltz time

FROM then on, Angus spent most of his spare time with Linda and the days that followed were the happiest she had ever known. They bathed together, played tennis, danced and explored the island, on happy, easy terms with each other. And sunny days were followed by warm, starlit nights to provide a halcyon background to their activities.

Perhaps it was, after all, a good thing that Angus had warned her to keep her head, she mused one evening as she dressed for dinner. Although she considered herself well-balanced, it would not be difficult to lose both head and heart in this beautiful island and in this hotel which so skilfully promoted an atmosphere of carefree enjoyment. It was indeed a rich diet after her plain Cornish life, and Angus was a stimulating, attractive companion. She liked his keen intelligence, and his honesty. And if his occasional arrogance challenged her, she enjoyed sparring with him, for he was a clever opponent and, as at tennis where he far outclassed her, she felt delighted when she scored a few points.

The chiffon dress was the colour of jade, with a long, full skirt that billowed lightly with every movement. It was the prettiest of all the dresses Mrs. Ferndale had chosen for her, and she saved it for Gala nights. That evening there was a Viennese dance, and she felt that the dress suited the occasion. She picked up the matching silk stole and silver evening bag, and wondered what her father would say if he could see her now. She hoped he would be happy in her enjoyment, but she wasn't at all sure.

She had a few minutes to spare before her rendezvous with Angus, and she pushed open the doors leading from her bedroom on to the tiny balcony. The sky was like black velvet, pricked with diamonds. The moon had not yet risen, but below her the scene was brilliant, for the flower-beds in the courtyard were floodlit, as were the two pools and the cascade between. On either side of the courtyard stood the tall royal palms, their leaves moving gently in the warm breeze. Beyond the palms lay the dark shape of the woods which fringed the golf course, and beyond the course, a thin dark silk strip which was the sea, broken by a faint creamy line of surf tumbling on the coral reef. If she pinched herself, she thought, she would wake up.

It was the custom at the hotel to have the main lounge candlelit in the evenings, romantic and flattering, but inconvenient, Angus said, when it came to tipping the boy who brought the drinks.

"I've collected such an assortment of American and British money that I need a good light to sort it out. I guess it won't be long before British currency is obsolete here," he observed.

"In the oldest British colony?"

"You wouldn't think so. Still, without American money, the island would be poor, and it's a bit far for the British tourist. How do you like that rum punch?"

"Delicious."

"This is a very seductive life. I shan't find it easy to go back."

"When will you be finished, Angus?"

"Another week."

"So soon?"

"It's taken longer than I anticipated."

"I shall be sorry when you go. Thank you for giving me such a lovely time."

"The enjoyment's been mutual. But there's another week yet. What's our singer got in store for us this evening?"

After a few preliminary ripples on the piano, the young woman began to sing a song from Bitter Sweet. It fitted Linda's mood, for the thought of Angus's departure had brought a chill to her heart.

Characteristically, after the singer had finished, Angus said briskly:

"She's better with modern stuff that doesn't call for much of a voice."

"This is to be an old-fashioned evening, specially designed to have a nostalgic appeal for our middle-aged visitors. It has an appeal for me, too."

"I'm in a pretty buttery state myself."

"What an admission! I promise not to take advantage of it."

Angus stood up as Ruth Elsted appeared by their table and said:

"Hullo, there."

"Join us for a drink," said Angus.

"Well, I'm really on my way back to the

office. We've a late session on tonight. But I'd like a few minutes off with you."

Angus ordered a rum punch for her, and discovering that she came from Virginia, which he knew well, they were soon talking happily together. When Angus took the trouble, he was good at putting people at their ease, drawing them out, thought Linda, watching them. Ruth's soft, southern accent was pleasing, and in the candlelight her pale face and cloudy dark hair took on an elusive charm. Although in her middle thirties, experienced and competent at her job, she yet had an appealing air of vulnerability. Tall and slender to the point of thinness, with small bones and undistinguished features apart from the large dark grey eyes, Ruth was neither pretty nor good-looking, but there was an indefinable charm about her personality which had drawn Linda to her. Perhaps it was because she offered such a contrast to the hard glitter of Mrs. Ferndale and the bored picture-book prettiness of Angela. Although Ruth talked so little about herself, Linda had the impression that her life had not been easy or happy,

and that a constant struggle against ill
health had dogged her.

When she left them to return to her
office, they went in to dinner. The tables
were arranged round a central dance space.

"I've never taken to this habit of dancing
between courses," said Angus, after he had
given their order. "Shall we wait until afterwards?"

"Yes, let's."

The meal, as always, was too extensive
for her appetite and she missed the last
course. With one foot tapping to the beat
of the waltz music, she wanted to be done
with food and to dance.

He was, as she had expected, a good
dancer, and they quickly found themselves
waltzing Viennese style in complete
harmony.

"You're very light. Nothing to you," he
said as he swung her round to the music of
the Gold and Silver Waltz.

She leaned back against his arm and
smiled up at him, her eyes shining.

"I'm air-borne. I still can't quite believe
in all this, you know."

"It's a hot-house atmosphere, all right.
Very intoxicating for the young. Perhaps

it's as well that the cost restricts it mainly to the middle-aged who've made their pile. They're not so likely to be carried off their feet. I'm not sure that you should be let loose in all this."

"I'm not, as a rule. The staff don't join in the social life. I'm being given a ball because you're here and your grandfather wanted me to sample it all."

"Well, you're sparkling like a firework under the treatment. I thought you were a very sober young creature when I saw you again last Easter. I'm glad the old sparks weren't permanently dimmed."

She clapped vigorously for an encore, and went into his arms again, radiantly happy, half in love with the dark face eyeing her with such a quizzical smile, her whole being responding to the lilt of the music. She wanted to go on waltzing with him for ever.

Towards the end of the evening, they went out on the terrace and had a long cold drink at a table by a group of date palms which moved gently in the breeze and gave an illusion of coolness. Roland came up to them as they were drinking.

"Hullo, there. Just thought I'd look in

and see that all was going well. Enjoying yourselves?"

"Very much," said Linda.

"Have a drink?" asked Angus.

"No, thanks. We've got some friends in at the bungalow this evening and I must get back. You're looking very attractive tonight, Linda."

"It's this flattering lighting out here."

"You're too modest. Keep an eye on her, Angus. We don't want to lose her valuable services to some rich American."

He gave them a friendly salute and strolled off. Angus made no comment. He seldom mentioned Roland or his step-mother, but Linda sensed the coolness he felt towards them. He seemed a little preoccupied, and she studied his profile with pleasure. Clean lines, nothing blurred about Angus. These few weeks in the sun had tanned him to near coffee colour. Black hair sleeked back, long straight nose, lean jawline. Long fingers and a slim hand for a man. She was conscious suddenly of every detail about him, flesh, bone, muscle; the fine cloth of his dinner jacket on the arm resting on the table, the gleam of the white shirtcuff, the patent leather shoe just brushing her skirt. Keep your head, she admonished herself, but when he turned and gave her an enquiring smile, her heart seemed to lurch in an uncontrollable fashion and her breath came quickly.

"You look starry-eyed. Grandfather would feel rewarded if he could see you."

"Tell him how much I'm enjoying myself, and how well you've discharged your duty."

"A duty, and a pleasure. You know that, don't you?"

"Yes."

"Come for a walk. I want to talk to you."

He took her arm and they walked through the courtyards, past the floodlit pools and cascade, until they came to a narrow wooden bridge spanning a chine on the outskirts of the hotel gardens. They leaned on it, looking back at the lighted façade of the hotel framed by its palm trees like an opal against the night sky. It was quiet here, the sound of the music barely reaching them above the rustling of palm leaves.

"I shall be extra busy next week and there may not be another opportunity to take stock, Lindey," he said, taking out his cigarette case.

"Don't talk about going. I'm Cinderella at the ball tonight, and I don't want to think about midnight."

"All these pleasures will still be available to you."

She was silent. Enjoyment only, he had said, and she had promised. But how could you promise not to lose your heart?

"I'm the one who's going back to London streets and traffic jams," he went on as she said nothing. "You'll be here for a year."

"Will you have to come out again?"

"I doubt it. I've got all I need to make a full report for my grandfather. It depends a bit on how he reacts to it. By the end of next week I shall have carried out my brief, though."

"So it will be a year before I see you again."

"Probably. A year can bring a lot of changes. Especially this year, to you. It's an entirely different life for you here. Will you seem a different person at the end of it? Or perhaps be married to a rich American, as Roland suggested, by then?"

"I don't think that's likely."

"I was a bit against this project of my grandfather's, you know. Not altogether happy about it even now."

"Why were you against it?"

"I didn't think my stepmother or my father would be suitable guides for an in-experienced girl in this sort of set-up."

She felt that he was choosing his words carefully, and smiled at what seemed an odd streak of old-fashioned puritanism in him.

"And now are you reassured that I'm mature enough to withstand the perils?"

"Not altogether, but you carry your own kind of armour, perhaps. What I wanted to say was this. I know we've just been enjoying ourselves, having a bit of fun, but . . . we've become close friends over these past weeks, haven't we?"

"Yes."

"What happens when you come home is another story. It would be foolish to look ahead. But the old days, when we were kids, and the present seem to have joined up into something pretty good. So, while you're here, will you write to me, Lindey?

Air mail comes very quickly and I want to keep in touch."

"So do I."

"And particularly, if any trouble crops up, no matter what kind, let me know."

"How ominous you make it sound, Angus! What sort of trouble do you think I'm likely to get into?"

"I feel you're out on a limb here. If you had any personal problems or difficulties, is there anyone here you could turn to for advice and help? My stepmother? My father? Any of your colleagues?"

"Well, no, I don't know any of them well enough. Peter Holmfield, perhaps. He's always very kind. Or Ruth. She'd be sympathetic, but not exactly a tower of strength. I've promised to write to your grandfather about any difficulties, but I can't see myself confiding any very personal matters to him."

"Well, then, do you trust me?"

"As myself," she said promptly, and for a moment silenced him. Then he said quietly:

"Thanks."

"And I'm delighted that you want me to write to you, and I shall keep you informed of all the perils that beset me," she said solemnly, her eyes dancing. "'Dear Angus,' I shall write, 'I am being pursued by an old wolf who has a fortune. I don't really love him, but he has a certain fascination for me. What shall I do?'"

"Keep your powder dry," said Angus, grinning. "You can stop needling my bossy habits."

"I'm not. It's nice of you to feel concerned. But you do forget I'm not a child, don't you? I really am a sober, responsible person, Angus."

"Maybe. But a shade unworldly, shall we say? Anyway, friendship doesn't flourish on long gaps, and letters will keep it going. Here's the address of my flat in London. A deal?"

"A deal," she said, tucking the card in her bag. "I hereby appoint you my father confessor."

"You're in a very mischievous mood. I'm not easily shocked, so you won't have to spare my blushes. Shall we seal the contract?"

She lifted her face and he kissed her, gently, without haste. She wanted to hold him then, but he released her quite deliberately and said:

"Well, Lindey Lou, do you want to dance again? We might be in time for the last waltz."

If he had felt her trembling in his arms, he gave no sign. She had promised to keep her head.

"Yes, let's dance it out," she said, and ran on ahead of him, her skirts brushing the bushes, unable to trust her voice any more.

And that was really the end of their fun together, for Angus worked all day and until late in the evening for the remainder of his time there, and she was not alone again with him until she went in the taxi to see him off at the airport, for once again his father and stepmother and Roland were otherwise engaged.

The formalities at the little airport were brief, and, after chatting away happily in the taxi about hotel matters, she found herself dumb at the moment of departure. A year seemed suddenly a very long time.

"Goodbye, Lindey Lou. Look after yourself. And don't forget our deal," he said, resting a hand on her shoulder a moment before picking up his brief-case.

"Goodbye, Angus. Thank you again for a wonderful time. I won't forget. Safe journey."

She stood outside the swing doors of the airport and watched him walk across the tarmac with the other travellers to the waiting monster, which had come from New York. It was the night flight, due in London at nine the next morning. He stopped at the top of the steps into the aircraft and waved, then disappeared. She stayed there, a prey to mixed emotions, as the huge jet moved slowly down to the runway, turned on to it, picked up speed, and in no time at all was rising swiftly over her head, lights winking. When it was out of sight, she returned slowly to the taxi. The bright holiday world was awaiting her. And if Angus's going left a larger blank than she cared to admit, she felt that the past weeks had established a friendship that would last. And just then, she asked no more.

11

Gossip

ANGELA walked slowly up the lane holding her husband's arm, the bored expression on her pretty face turning to petulance as she saw Linda running down a steep slope of the golf course as nimbly as a fawn, her arms wide, her hair blowing back from her face, the thin material of her blue and white dress flattened against her slender figure. Behind her, at a more decorous pace, came Peter Holmfield carrying a polythene bag.

"I'm sick of looking like an old tug," burst out Angela, her eyes on Linda.

"Never mind, puss. Only another month, and you'll be a sylph again."

"It seems endless. And I'm bored, bored, bored with it."

"I'll take you away for a really good holiday afterwards."

"Where? I'm tired of this sort of place."

"What about Paris?"

134

"That's better. What on earth's Peter Holmfield got in that polythene bag, do you suppose?"

"Wild flowers, probably. He's helping Linda make a collection, I believe."

"That's what they say," said Angela spitefully. She felt affronted by that free, lithe figure.

"Any other ideas?"

"Enid says she's sure Peter's having an affair with someone."

"Are you and Mrs. Holmfield on cosy Christian name terms now? You know it's not wise to get too friendly with staff, Angie."

"I know, and I don't, but I must have *someone* to talk to or I'll go mad. And Enid's good company."

"What about me?"

"You have to spend so much time at the club-house, and I don't like going there now I'm like this. Besides, I like to have some feminine company just now."

"Well, don't let her scare you with old wives' tales about childbirth. And don't ever discuss hotel business with her. Now what's all this about Peter Holmfield?"

135

"I don't think I'll tell you, since you're so sniffy about Enid."

Roland looked down at her pouting lips, and smiled. Drawing her to the side of the lane, he kissed her and ran his fingers round her neck.

"Poor puss. You're a bit sorry for yourself just now, and no wonder. I'll make it up afterwards, I promise. But between ourselves, I'd say our Mrs. Holmfield is a bossy, possessive type, wouldn't you? If I were her husband, I might be tempted to seek a little sugar elsewhere. She's marvellous at managing the maids, but that quality's not so appealing in a wife. I like them feminine and clinging," he added, putting his arm round Angela's shoulder as they walked on.

"Well, she is bossy," said Angela, mollified, "but Peter Holmfield's a bit feeble and probably needs managing. Anyway, I hold no brief for a man who deceives his wife."

"What makes her think he is?"

"Several things. Unexplained absences. Lipstick she found on his collar. I tell you, she's getting really steamed up about it. Do you suppose it might be Linda? I've seen

136

them together several times, and I wouldn't put it past her."

"She's warm enough. Made a good deal of headway with Angus when he was here, and he's no easy conquest. Could be, my little puss," said Roland thoughtfully.

"She's probably making up for all the time she lost in Cornwall. Grandpa's innocent, indeed! I think she needs watching, Roland. She could make trouble."

"You may be right. Think you ought to turn back now? Don't want to overdo it."

"I suppose so," said Angela, sighing. "The days seem so long and empty. I just don't think I'm the maternal type."

"Spend the time thinking what you'd like me to buy you in Paris."

"What's the limit?" she asked, her cheeks dimpling.

"I'd like to say the sky, but Grandfather's salary scale isn't all that generous," said Roland, with an edge to his voice.

"And he's got all that money. And you work so hard."

"The old man doesn't rank a sports manager as a worker. It's more a pleasant hobby for me, he thinks. Anyway, puss, you shall have just whatever you want in

Paris. After all, Grandpa will have a new grandchild. He might well offer to pay for the Paris trip himself. We shall both have earned a break, I guess. I'll be home to lunch. May not go back this afternoon. We'll have a siesta together in the garden."

"I've got a nice husband," said Angela, lifting her face for his kiss.

"So you have. I'm not grumbling, either. If you hear any more rumblings from Enid Holmfield, let me know, darling. Don't want trouble among the staff."

He watched her walk back along the lane towards the bungalow until she disappeared round the bend, then walked on towards the golf club-house, his face thoughtful.

Half-way through the morning, he went across to the hotel and sought out his mother. He found her giving instructions to the woman who looked after the flower arrangements.

"If you're breaking for coffee, Mother, I'll join you. Something I think might interest you."

"Of course, dear. Private?"

"Yes."

"Let's have it in my sitting-room, then."

He waited until the maid had brought

them coffee there, then repeated his wife's tale about Enid Holmfield.

"True, do you think?" she asked, her eyes alert.

"That Peter Holmfield's straying? Yes, I think it's likely. I've twice seen him coming away from the beach hut lateish. Once, he said he'd come out for a stroll, but I had the impression that he was a bit nervous. The second time, I was some way away, but I'm sure it was Peter and there was a woman with him. They separated at the golf course."

"Linda?"

"Too far away to recognise who it was. Could have been. I dismissed it. None of my business, I thought. Anyway, there was nothing concrete to go on. Thought you might like to know about it. Grandpa wouldn't exactly approve of his protégée carrying on an affair with a married man."

"And I can't afford to have Enid Holmfield upset. She's more valuable to me than anybody on the domestic staff. A splendid manageress. Leave this with me, Roland. Don't discuss it with anybody, except Angela, of course. I shan't say anything to Austin at this stage. I'll handle it. Just keep me posted."

"I will. When's Mr. Ferndale coming here? Have you heard?"

"He suggested the beginning of September, but I've asked him to make it the end of the month, when he'll be able to see your baby. Don't want him arriving in the middle of it all."

"No reaction yet to Angus's report?"

"He says he'll discuss it with us when he comes."

"Full of schemes for reorganising, I suppose, to screw some more profit out of it. Darned cheek calling in Angus at all. Our own accountants here are competent enough. It makes me boil. The way we run this place, carry all the responsibility, and yet the old man owns it. He should have given it to Father in the first place."

"My dear, he's the sort of man who can never relinquish the reins. He must rule. But he's seventy-eight, remember. We can humour him in his old age."

"But we've no guarantee that the place will ever be ours. It's so unjust. And he's as tight as a clam about the future."

"He has only his family to leave his

money to, and he's not the man to let it go out of the family. Austin is his only son, Harriet his only daughter."

"And Angus?"

"We can discount Angus, I think. Mr. Ferndale said he'd disinherit him when he chose to go his own way instead of joining the family business. He's a man of his word. There's still no love lost between them. You can take my word for that."

"But he sent him out here to investigate."

"Mr. Ferndale uses good brains for his own benefit, wherever they belong," said Cynthia drily.

"And Linda? He seems to count her as one of the family, though I'm blessed if I know why."

"Yes. I've thought about Linda. He does seem to show a more than godfatherly interest in her future. But I have an idea this is his testing ground for her. I don't think, somehow, she's going to come out of it very creditably. Old Mr. Ferndale is a puritan. Some things he would not stomach. I'm not altogether surprised at your news today. I think that girl's a dark horse."

"She's ripened up out here very quickly. Really made the pace with Angus, I thought. Haven't made much headway with her myself, but she seems thick enough with Peter. Wild flowers! Well, that's one way of putting it."

"She didn't lose much time in getting in touch with her godfather after her father died, either. She's got an eye on the main chance, all right. However, we mustn't jump to conclusions about Peter Holmfield. Just wait and keep our ears and eyes open. She'll trip herself up, in time. I don't think Mrs. Holmfield is the type of woman to take an affair of this sort lying down."

"Nor I. Poor Peter," said Roland, grinning.

"Poor Peter, nonsense. He should remember he's a husband and a father. A decent enough man, really, I think. He's being led on, no doubt. Now, my dear, I must pack you off. I've a cocktail party with the new guests this morning. Is Angela all right? I haven't seen her lately."

"Fed up with waiting. We'll be glad when it's all over."

"Yes. I hope she gives the old man

another grandson. That would please him. Take good care of her, dear."

After Roland had left her, Cynthia lingered by the window a few minutes, her mind busy. This was what she had been waiting for. A chance to unseat this interloper. She was not really concerned with the likelihood of Linda behaving like this. She wanted it to be true, and therefore it was true. If she played her cards carefully, she could have Linda Dawley removed from the Ferndale family once and for all. This was just the sort of thing old Mr. Ferndale would never tolerate. Patience, she thought. Go carefully.

Descending in the lift, she picked up her husband on a lower floor.

"Hullo, my dear," he said. "On the way to entertain the ladies?"

"Correct."

"You're looking in dazzling form."

"I feel it. Really on the ball today."

"Wish I could gate-crash. I've a session with Holmfield over the accounts. Not nearly such a pleasant prospect."

"You wouldn't really enjoy our little hen-party. Anyway, I'm not sure that I'd let you loose among them. Far too handsome," she said, pleased at the admiration in his eyes.

"I know when I'm lucky. You look as though you've won a football pool this morning. Are you holding out on me?"

She patted his cheek and smiled as they reached the ground floor.

"You'd be surprised," she said, and walked swiftly across the the hall to her rendezvous in the Welcome Bar.

Austin watched her go. Her slender, upright back view might have belonged to a girl of twenty instead of a woman in her mid-forties. He still found himself surprised at having captured this attractive woman for his wife eight years ago. Not only physically attractive, but capable, too. And if he felt irritated sometimes by the realisation that she was humouring him, she did it so charmingly that he could scarcely complain.

12

Bird on the wing

ON the steep, sandy slope leading from the golf course to the beach, two green lizards were fighting. Linda, sitting on the grassy edge above, watched them, fascinated. They would retreat, remain motionless for a few moments, then dart at each other in a flash. It was dusk, and the beach was taking on a rosy sheen as the sun went down. She still found it mildly surprising that the lovely sunny days should not be succeeded by the long light evenings of the English summer, but here dusk came down swiftly soon after tea.

There was a shout behind her, and young David Holmfield ran up, followed by his father. From his hand dangled two pairs of wet swimming trunks, with which he caressed Linda's bare neck.

"Ow! Monkey!" exclaimed Linda,

laughing, as she dodged away from them. "Have a good swim?"

"Super. Daddy took me right out, beyond the surf."

"He's getting to be quite a good swimmer," said Peter Holmfield.

"See those lizards, David," said Linda, and they all three spent the next ten minutes following the battle until the lizards tired and disappeared into the nearby scrub.

Under her hand, the boy's shoulder felt small and bony. He was a thin tadpole of a boy with fair hair and the face of a blue-eyed cherub masking a lively, mischievous temperament. He was affectionate too, and adored his father. He and Linda had become good friends, and on the previous afternoon she had taken him on the bus to the zoo. With both parents occupied all day, he found the school holidays apt to drag, and he had welcomed Linda's outings during the past month.

"How's the botanical collection coming on?" asked Peter Holmfield.

"Very well. I packed up the notes and all the specimens I'd collected and pressed, and sent them off to Mr. Brookwood yesterday."

"Have you been to the botanical garden yet?"

"No. I mean to go there next week. I seem to have so little spare time and so much to see."

"I'm hungry, Dad," announced David. "Let's go home."

"Righto. You coming our way, Linda?"

"Of course she is. Come on, lazybones," said David, and gave her a vigorous push that caught her by surprise and sent her sliding down the sandy cliff on her back.

"David!" exclaimed his father, but the boy had danced away.

"I'll hide on the way back. See if you can find me," he called.

"I'll find you, and wallop you, my boy," said his father, plunging down the cliff to give Linda a hand in her climb up.

She was breathless when she reached the top again, for the slope was not far off vertical. David was out of sight.

"He's as lively as a squib today. I'll give him a talking-to when I get hold of him. Here, let me brush you down," said Peter.

Her back was covered with sand from

the slide down. Peter was brushing it off when his wife appeared round the bend. The bus from Hamilton had deposited her at the golf-course stop, and she was taking the short cut across to their bungalow. She was carrying two shopping bags, and stopped dead as she saw them. Neither Linda nor Peter saw her at first. When Peter had cleared most of the sand from Linda's back, he half turned to shake his drill trousers free of sand, and saw his wife.

"Hullo, Enid. Have a good shop?"

"Yes. Where's David?"

"Hiding somewhere. He's too lively by half today. Pushed Linda down the cliff."

"I thought you were going swimming."

"We did. We're just on our way home."

There was something in Mrs. Holmfield's attitude that made Linda feel uncomfortable, and she said:

"Well, I must be getting back. Can I give you a hand with those shopping bags, Mrs. Holmfield?"

"No, thanks. Peter will take them."

Linda hesitated, then said goodbye and departed, bearing off to the left of their route, although normally she would have

followed the path round by the staff bunga-
lows.

Back at the hotel, she found two letters
awaiting her. One was from old Mr.
Ferndale, saying that he was looking
forward to seeing her at the end of the
month. The other was from Angus, which
made her forget the uncomfortable little
meeting with Enid Holmfield.

I shall be coming out with Grandfather
for a conference on the implementation
of the recommendations in my report on
the hotel. Can't spare more than a week,
but that should give us a chance to get
acquainted again.

Your letters, though welcome, are
factual without really telling me much
about one Linda Dawley. Why the
reticence?

I've told Grandfather that his Cinderella has blossomed amazingly under the
treatment, thus confirming the sound-
ness of his project and the absurdity of
my doubts, a very satisfactory state of
affairs. Not that Grandfather ever needs
confirmation that he is right. He is

looking forward very much to seeing you.

So am I.

Yours,
Angus

Delighted at the prospect of seeing Angus again, she read the letter twice before tucking it away in her bag. Why the reticence? It was true that when she wrote to him, she was careful to keep her feelings under lock and key, inhibited still by that conversation she had overheard between him and his aunt, and his warning to her against losing her heart. All he had revealed was a wish to remain friends, and that wish seemed to be based chiefly on his desire to act as a guide and counsellor to a foolish child whose head was only too likely to be turned by the glamorous world she had been shot into.

Nothing could dim her pleasure at the prospect of seeing her mentor again, however, and her high spirits were infectious when, the next day, she took a picnic lunch with Ruth Elsted to a little cove on the other side of the island, where they bathed and lazed and bathed again in the rolling surf of that dazzling blue sea.

"You look so happy that it hurts," said Ruth unexpectedly, after a long pause during which Linda had been gazing out to sea, her hands clasped round her knees. "What are you thinking about?"

"Just how lovely the world is. Look at that sea and the surf breaking on the coral reef. And the pink sand, and the casuarina trees on the promontory. I feel part of it all today."

"Hold on to it. Happiness is an elusive bird. Cherish every little moment of it."

Linda turned, surprised at the unusual vehemence in her friend's soft voice.

"I do. Have you found it so elusive, Ruth?"

"Oh, not more than most people, I guess."

"Did you have a happy childhood?"

"Reasonably so, until I had a bicycle accident when I was ten, and spent the next six years in and out of hospital having operations to put me together again."

"And then?"

"My mother died. She'd been so splendid, nursing me, keeping my courage up. My father had died when I was a baby and she'd had a struggle. It seemed hard that just as I was getting stronger and might have been able to help her instead of being a burden, she died."

"Poor Ruth."

"Well, let's not spoil the day by looking back. Live in the present. Take each hour as it comes. And when it's a happy one, try to hold it back."

"Have you always done secretarial work?"

"Yes. This is the best job I've ever had, though. Mr. Ferndale's kind and considerate, and I love this climate. Pleasant living quarters and comfort all around me. What more could a woman ask?"

But Linda could never quite escape from the sense of an underlying sadness in her friend. It was nothing tangible, for Ruth, although retiring and reserved, was never miserable, never complained. It was an aura she carried with her. Something to do with her fragile appearance, perhaps, and those large dark eyes in the thin face.

"You've been with Mr. Ferndale ever since the hotel began, haven't you?"

"Yes. I've enjoyed seeing it develop into what it is today."

"Never been tempted to marry?"

"No. At thirty-five, I'm happy to accept my lot as a spinster. Even if anyone wanted to marry me, I'd be a poor bargain. I can't have children and I'd be a rotten housewife. I like my life here, anyway. It suits me."

"And you want to stay here always? Never go back home?"

"I don't look back or ahead," said Ruth lightly. "Live in the present. 'Unborn tomorrow and dead yesterday, why fret about them if today be sweet!'"

"You like Omar Khayyám? I might have guessed.

Come fill the Cup, and in the fire of Spring
The winter garment of Repentance fling:
The Bird of Time has but a little way
To fly—and Lo! the Bird is on the Wing.

My father used to roll out those verses to me when I was very young, and I can hear him now. He had a lovely voice for poetry."

"He was a poet, wasn't he? Tell me about him."

Walking back, still talking about poetry, pleased to have discovered this mutual love, Linda interrupted her friend to point out two catbirds in the hibiscus hedge. These little birds, blue as delphinium flowers, charmed her with their odd cat-like calls. Now, as the sun went down, to see them darting among the pink and red blossoms of the hibiscus gave her a stab of delight. Then, with a vivid flash of wings, they had gone.

"Lo, the bird is on the wing. Brief as happiness," said Ruth.

"I'm not going to let Omar's melancholy cast a shadow over a splendid day," said Linda, feeling confident and joyful in the knowledge that in three weeks she would be seeing Angus, and in the belief that life was not only good now, but full of promise for the future.

13

Alien country

PETER HOLMFIELD hovered by the reception desk while Linda dealt with the American.

"The confirmation came through this morning, Captain Lock. Three reservations on the night flight on the thirtieth. Would you see them in the Hamilton office about the exchange as soon as possible?"

"I'm much obliged. That's a weight off my mind. Now we can relax and enjoy ourselves, son."

The boy beside him gave him a grin and took his hand as they walked out. He was about six or seven years old, red-haired and freckled, with his father's pale blue eyes. Linda looked after them, feeling sorry for the burly man with the good-natured face and the tired eyes. She had learned that his wife had recently died, leaving him with the boy and a girl of four. Before rejoining his regiment in the far east, he was taking the children to England to his wife's parents, and as the day of his recall had been brought forward, he had had to change the air-tickets. There was something helpless and touching about the man's clumsy efforts to cope with his family responsibilities, and she had been as helpful as she could.

"Hullo, Peter," she said, turning to him with a smile. "What can I do for you?"

"David says you've promised to play cricket on the beach with him this afternoon."

"Correct. In a rash moment, I yielded. If it's too hot, I hope he'll settle for a bathe instead."

"I wanted to make sure he's not being a nuisance. You've been so good with him during the holidays, but I feel you might prefer a more restful occupation than cricket in your time off."

"David's no trouble. I enjoy his company. Anyway, school starts again tomorrow."

"Thank goodness! Holidays are much too long. Anyway, thanks for being so good to the boy. You're a great favourite with him, but don't let him abuse his luck."

Peter gave her his kind, winning smile, so much like David's, and went off to his office as a party came up to enquire about fishing trips.

The day was warm, and the breeze that usually tempered the heat and made the climate so delightful was less evident, so that Linda found the charms of cricket, never overwhelming where she was concerned, diminishing rapidly as the afternoon wore on. When Peter turned up soon after five, she happily relinquished her role of bowler to him.

"I'm going to have a siesta over by the rocks there," she said. "David's legs may be inexhaustible, but mine aren't."

"Here, take this for a pillow," said Peter, stripping off his linen jacket and throwing it to her. "Now, my lad. Let's see how you cope with spin bowling."

Linda made her way to the rocks at the end of the cove and sat down thankfully, propping herself up on one elbow to watch them for a few minutes. David looked absurdly small, lashing out rather wildly to his father's tempting balls. Soon, Peter was batting and David making ferocious runs to deliver balls that had a habit of burying themselves short in the sand. She smiled, rolled Peter's jacket up for a pillow, stretched herself flat on the warm sand and left them to it. In fifteen more days, she would see Angus. They could not go quickly enough.

That was the evening when Angela's daughter came tardily into the world, and a few days later Linda went to the nursing home to see her and take some candies and flowers. She found Angela a little depressed, and strangely apathetic about the baby, who stared at Linda with solemn blue eyes and seemed contented to have arrived in the world. During her visit, when she was seeking for something cheerful to talk about, for she never found it easy to talk to Angela, Mrs. Holmfield came in, and when she saw Linda, her face took on a hostile expression so naked and fierce that it struck Linda dumb.

"As you've already got Miss Dawley for company, I won't stay, Angela. Just wanted to bring you some magazines."

"Oh, do stay, Enid. There's no limit to the number of visitors I can have. Anyway, Linda's just going, aren't you, Linda?"

"Yes," said Linda, who had intended to

stay longer, thinking the girl needed cheering up. "I must be going."

She said goodbye, and felt their eyes following her out of the room. Waiting for the bus back to the hotel, she felt shaken by that encounter. It was enmity she had seen in Mrs. Holmfield's face, but she could not imagine why. She had seen little of her during her months at the hotel, for they worked in different spheres. Surely she did not resent the time she had spent with David? He was at a loose end in the holidays, with his mother occupied all day. Perhaps she should have asked her permission, but she had always had Peter's approval for their jaunts.

It worried her for a few days, and then, so happy was her mood, she dismissed it as imagination. Angela came home a week later, and Roland and his mother organised a party at the bungalow to celebrate the occasion. Linda was not invited, but was not altogether surprised. It was her evening on duty, but since she and Jean were always willing to change over if any special occasion cropped up for either of them, it would have been easy for her to have been free for the family celebration, but nothing was said. Ever since she had come here, she had been treated as any other employee, kept at a distance from the Ferndale family. Angus was right. She could never have turned to any of them for help or advice.

At the end of her spell of duty on the night of the party, she felt restless. With a headache hovering, she decided on a stroll before going to bed. The nights were beautiful, warm and enticing, and the long drive and the walks round the hotel were popular with guests until midnight and after. Couples sat in arbours, leaned on low walls of terraces, strolled arm in arm, a star-pricked sky above, the rustle of palms around them, the scent of oleanders in the air.

Linda walked slowly along the terrace where bougainvillaea tumbled down the wall, a glowing mass of red and gold in the floodlighting, then she turned away from the lights and took the path which wound through the rock garden, where aloes stood out starkly, their spear-like leaves dark and cruel in the pale moonlight. It brought her out to the lane which led to the hotel beach. The tall hibiscus hedges each side seemed to hem her in, and she left the lane through a gap just before reaching the beach, and climbed up to a ridge where a seat under a group of casuarina trees invited her to linger. The wash of the surf on the pale sand below made pleasing music, and she leaned back against the tree, feeling the warm breeze stir her hair and play with her dress. Three more days, and Angus would be here, and the repetition of this theme song in her heart for the past weeks made it impossible to deny the hold he now had on her feelings. What had he meant, that night after the dance? Friendship, and no more? He had not committed himself, but she had felt the warmth of his concern for her.

Trapped in thoughts of Angus, she had no idea how long had elapsed since she left the hotel. It was only a sound from the direction of the beach hut that recalled her to the present. Too muffled by the song of the surf to register clearly, it might have been a shutter flapping. There would be nobody there at this time. She lingered for a few moments longer, but her dreamy mood was broken, and she made her way back, walking more briskly now. In the lane, she thought she heard footsteps behind her, but when she turned, the lane was empty. She was not a nervous person, but nevertheless found herself hurrying, and she was not sorry when she reached the lighted drive of the hotel. There were few people about and, glancing at her watch, she was amazed to find that it was well past midnight.

She was half-way up the drive when Mr. Ferndale's car passed her, and she met them in the hall. Cynthia Ferndale was wearing a cream silk suit, and her diamond brooch and ear-rings flashed as she turned. She held a mink stole loosely round her shoulders as she regarded Linda steadily above her smiling lips.

"Hullo, Linda. You're very late."

"Yes. I had a headache, and went for a stroll. It's such a beautiful night. Did you enjoy the party?"

"Very much. I think it cheered Angela up. She was looking her old self tonight."

"Has the headache gone?" asked Austin kindly, as they waited at the lift.

"Yes, thank you."

In the lift, there was a constrained silence. The Ferndales got out on the second floor, leaving Linda to ascend to her loftier station. For the first time, she felt

162

homesick; found the prospect of a whole year here less attractive than she had thought. For all the glamour and luxury of her surroundings, and the variety of her daily life, it seemed to her now to lack warmth. She felt in alien country.

The lift doors closed behind her and she walked down the impersonal, carpeted corridor to her little room at the end. The holiday feast was beginning to cloy; she would welcome a plainer diet.

The air conditioning in her room was faulty, and it was hot in there. She flung the windows wider and stood on the balcony, looking out over the garden and the pools and the cascade, and the stately royal palms with their plumes moving gently against the sky. For all the beauty of the scene, she found herself thinking of autumn evenings at home, the leaves beginning to change colour, bonfires, the first white frost and fireside evenings. Cold nights and hot water bottles. People there would think her mad to envy them. Perhaps she was. But it called her then, the English countryside, climate and all. Travellers' joy and purple brambles in the hedgerows, shining conkers in the lane under the chestnut tree, the hips and hawthorn berries, and, loveliest of all, the pink, translucent berries hanging like little lamps on the yew trees. The robin's plaintive autumn song. The blustery south-west wind that smelt of the sea and set the leaves whirling. The crisp, cold air of a clear night, heralding frost. She loved it all.

And home was where Angus was.

14

The web

"I TELL you, Mrs. Ferndale, either that girl goes, or I go," declared Enid Holmfield, her eyes blazing, her thin-featured face white and tense.

"Now sit down, Mrs. Holmfield, and we'll talk about it calmly. You say that Linda Dawley is too friendly with your husband."

"That's putting it mildly. She's enticing him away from me. I've known something was up for a long time, but I couldn't find out who it was. Now I know."

"How do you know?"

"I've seen them out together a lot. Oh, she's clever. She's used David as a cover. I might not have suspected her if your daughter-in-law hadn't remarked on the time she and Peter spend together looking for wild flowers. A likely story! Then I found them together on the cliffs. He was brushing the sand off her. They'd sent David off on his own."

"It's not very conclusive, Mrs. Holmfield."

"I've found her hair on his jacket. Nobody else I know has chestnut hair. And they meet at the beach hut late at night. Peter always has been a one for taking walks in the evening before going to bed, but I'm too tired at the end of the day. He says he has a sedentary job and the exercise is good for him. I'm on my feet all day. It seemed reasonable enough until it got later and later before he got back. One night, I went out to look for him. I met him in the lane leading from the beach hut."

"Alone?"

"Yes. But I'd seen a woman crossing the golf course a few minutes before I met him. She was hurrying and I swear she wasn't a visitor, but she was too far away to recognise. I didn't say anything, but last night I went to the beach hut a bit earlier and waited. I didn't think anybody was in there, as it was dark, and I expected to see them come. I hid in the shrubs just behind. But they must have been there all the time, because a torch came on and I heard the door squeak, and voices, then the lock turning. I started to run but tripped over a root. By the time I'd scrambled down, I saw Peter's back disappearing round the rocks at the end of the beach. The girl had vanished but I thought I heard footsteps in the lane. I ran up the lane, and saw her. It was Linda Dawley. She turned. Perhaps she heard me. Anyway, I kept in under the hedge where it was dark and she didn't see me, but I saw her plainly in the moon-light."

"I see."

Cynthia's voice was thoughtful and her face was masked.

"You don't believe me? She may be a relative of yours, Mrs. Ferndale, and be in a privileged position, but I'm not having any loose girl break up my marriage. She goes, or we go. Peter will leave with me. He'd never give up David."

"I do believe you, Mrs. Holmfield. I met Linda when she got back to the hotel last night. It was very late and I was surprised that she'd been out on her own at that hour. Did you say anything to your husband when you got home?"

"He didn't come in until some time after

167

I was back. He must have come the long way round the coast. But I was waiting for him. We had a row. He denied it all, of course. Then I decided to come to you. It's probably more her fault than his. She's led him on, and men are . . ." Enid Holmfield shrugged her shoulders as though little could be expected of men in such circumstances.

"Quite," said Cynthia. "This is a very unpleasant business, Mrs. Holmfield. I'm sorry. I'm in a difficult position, too. Linda Dawley is no relative, but she is the goddaughter of old Mr. Ferndale, who owns this hotel. It was his idea that she should have a spell here, and I shall have to give him very conclusive evidence to justify removing her."

"It's conclusive enough, isn't it? And I'm not going to whitewash it, whoever she is. Shameless and wicked, I call it. A married man with a child. Privileged she may be, but it's her or us."

"Old Mr. Ferndale will certainly not condone such behaviour, I can assure you, once he's convinced of the truth of your accusations. You'll have to repeat to him what you have told me. He's due here on

Friday. Until then, will you say nothing about this to anybody? Just leave it to me. I should be very sorry indeed to lose your services, Mrs. Holmfield. You know that. I think I can promise you that it won't come to that. Meanwhile, I hope I can count on your discretion, for all our sakes. Make no approach to Linda, and keep it to yourself. I'll handle it."

"Very well, Mrs. Ferndale."

"You've no idea how your husband got hold of the beach hut key, I suppose? It's locked at six each night and there are only two keys. Benjie has one, and I'm not sure where the spare is kept."

"The reception desk might know," said Enid Holmfield drily.

"Yes. Well, I'm glad you came to me, Mrs. Holmfield. You did the right thing. I shall take the necessary steps to see that this state of affairs is stopped. I repeat, don't discuss it with anybody, and leave it to me. I shall want you to see old Mr. Ferndale when he comes. And I shall have a talk with your husband today."

"Very well, Mrs. Ferndale. But that girl goes, or I do," with which venomous remark, Enid Holmfield left.

Cynthia spent the next half hour thinking the matter over. Two cigarettes and a cup of coffee later, she telephoned the accounts office and asked Peter Holmfield to come and see her. When he arrived she gave him a reassuring smile, but studied him carefully as he sat down. He looked tired and worried, as well he might be, she thought. He was a good-looking man, well built, with blunt but pleasant features, abundant sandy hair, good blue eyes, a kindly manner. In his mid-thirties, he did not look the straying type. But Enid Holmfield, intense, possessive, jealous, was not exactly a cosy little woman. Weighing him up, she played her cards accordingly.

"Your wife came to see me this morning, Mr. Holmfield, with a very disturbing ultimatum. Either I dismiss Linda Dawley, or you and she go. I don't think I have to go into the reason, do I?"

"I didn't think Enid would go that far, although she threatened to," he said slowly. "It's quite untrue, Mrs. Ferndale. There's nothing between Linda and me but a quite innocent friendship. She's been very good to David. It's absurd of Enid to jump to such conclusions."

170

"She does have some evidence for her conclusions. But I don't want to go into all that. I'm quite ready to believe that your wife may be seeing things in a blacker light than is justified, but these visits to the beach hut at night are not exactly to your credit. I don't know how you got hold of the key, but I must ask you to return it to me. Have you got it on you?"

"No."

"Then let me have it some time today."

"Of course. Linda knows nothing about it."

"Come, Mr. Holmfield. I don't blame you for trying to protect her, but I'm afraid your wife's evidence makes your denial gallant but unconvincing. Don't look so worried. I'm prepared to give you the benefit of the doubt and say that this is no more than a foolish escapade. But, since your wife will certainly not let it rest there, but will raise a scandal and blacken Linda's reputation before leaving and taking you with her, I think it would be kinder to Linda to admit to a certain foolishness with her. The consequences won't be nearly so damaging to her as your wife's tongue, if nothing is done. And if your wife left I assume that you would go with her. You have your son to consider."

"Of course. But why should Linda lose her job, because that is what it means, I suppose?"

"It was only a temporary arrangement, anyway. Her godfather, old Mr. Ferndale, never meant her to stay permanently."

"Linda has done absolutely nothing she could be blamed for. Enid has misconstrued the whole business."

"You mean it wasn't Linda who was with you in the beach hut, although your wife saw her walking away from it last night?"

"No."

"Then who was it?"

"I was alone."

"Now you're not making things easy for me or for yourself. I think you must really give up this gallant determination to protect Linda, because you'll do her more harm by denying it than admitting it."

"How?"

"If you admit it, I shall make light of it to old Mr. Ferndale. He's devoted to Linda, and very indulgent. I shall have to tell him of your wife's ultimatum, and suggest that in view of the awkward situation that has arisen, it might be advisable to cut Linda's time here short. It's a simple way out of a dangerous situation. Whatever the truth, your wife is convinced that you and Linda are having an affair and she won't put up with having Linda here. I don't want to lose either of you. For Linda, it's different. She is the protégée of a wealthy man, and this job has really only been a kind of finishing school for her. It won't be any hardship to her. If you persist in denying it, the consequences could be serious for Linda, you, and your wife and child. You know your wife. She left me in no doubt that she would stop at nothing. Jealousy can be very cruel to all parties."

Peter Holmfield looked at his hands and was silent for a few moments. Then he looked up and said quietly:

"I really have no choice, have I?"

"No."

"I don't see why Mr. Ferndale or anybody else has to be told. Why not say that Linda's tired of the job? Or not really needed now that the quiet season is coming on?"

"That is not very practical. But you must leave that side of it to me. I promise you that it will only be treated as a foolish escapade, but Mr. Ferndale must be given a sound enough reason for Linda's removal. You'll have to admit to a certain foolish indiscretion, but I'll make as light of it as possible."

"I don't like it."

"And, believe me, nor do I. Any of it," said Cynthia sharply. "I offer this as the easiest solution to a very nasty problem, and I think you should be grateful to get out of it so easily. Your wife could, and would, make Linda's life unbearable. I have forbidden her to approach Linda, but only because I promised to deal with this matter myself. But if Linda remains, your wife's tongue would be unrestrained. Quite frankly, I wouldn't want Linda exposed to it, whatever foolishness she's been up to. And you and your wife would have to find another job, for her threat was no idle one. We should all be the losers."

"Yes. I'm sorry, Mrs. Ferndale. This has been very upsetting. Your way is best."

"You'll admit it, then? I'll put it in as good a light as I can."

"Very well."

"If I can keep you off the scene, I will,

but it may not be possible. Meanwhile, please keep away from Linda."

"I understand."

"Don't worry. It will all prove a storm in a tea-cup, if we behave sensibly," said Cynthia in a more kindly tone, for she recognised him as her strongest ally.

When he had gone, she sat back and thought out her approach to her father-in-law the next day. Really, she thought, things couldn't have turned out better. Luke Ferndale was nothing if not a puritan. She did not envy Linda Dawley. However, she'd asked for it. The evidence was more conclusive than she had dared hope. The next thing was to tell her husband and Roland, and make sure that they handled it her way. Whatever reorganisation the old man would want to impose in the light of Angus's report, they could safely bank on one welcome change: the removal of Linda Dawley from the hotel and the Ferndale family circle.

15

Prisoner at the bar

"WELL, that was very welcome," said Luke Ferndale, putting down his empty cup and leaning back in the armchair. "I'm sorry Linda had to be in Hamilton this afternoon, Austin. I'd hoped she would have been at the airport to meet us."

"I had to send her in to the bank, Father. My secretary is off ill, and nobody else could be spared."

"When will she be back?"

"Any time now. But before you see her, there's something we have to tell you." Austin glanced at his wife, hesitating, his manner embarrassed.

"Something to tell me?" Luke looked up sharply. "Nothing wrong, is there?"

Austin and Roland both looked at Cynthia. Angus eyed them warily as he lit a cigarette.

"I'm really awfully sorry about this,"

said Cynthia gently. "I'm afraid it's going to upset you, and I had intended to postpone telling you until tomorrow because I thought you'd be tired after the journey, but if I don't tell you now, someone else might, and perhaps it's better to get it over with."

"Well, get on with it," said Luke testily. "Linda's all right, isn't she?"

"Yes." Cynthia looked at her hands.

"You can't dress it up, Mother," said Roland. "The plain truth is, Linda's been carrying on an affair with Peter Holmfield, his wife's found out, and is raising Cain."

"Linda and Holmfield?" said Luke, incredulous.

"Yes. I'm afraid it's true," said Cynthia. "It's come as a great shock. I only heard about it two days ago, when Mrs. Holmfield came to me and said that either Linda must leave this hotel, or she and her husband would. Then she told me what had been going on."

"What grounds had she got for believing it?" asked Angus drily.

Cynthia repeated every detail of Enid Holmfield's story. It sounded very

177

convincing. Luke's face was grim as he said:

"If this is true, it's a disgraceful state of affairs. I can hardly credit it. Are you sure Mrs. Holmfield isn't exaggerating, Cynthia? You had no suspicion, and yet you've been keeping an eye on Linda."

"I've done my best, but Linda's not a child. This is a big hotel, and it's not easy to keep track of all that goes on."

"But you never thought Linda capable of this sort of behaviour?"

"Well," Cynthia hesitated, then went on delicately. "I did hear rumours some weeks ago, and, to be really honest, I *have* been a little worried by a certain . . . Well, Linda did seem to me to be a little too easy-going with men, but I thought I might be a bit old-fashioned for these days. I was brought up in a more disciplined age. When I heard these rumours, I decided to give Linda the benefit of the doubt and dismiss them as gossip."

"Who was spreading the rumours?"

"Oh, there were just remarks, dropped here and there. I should have taken them more seriously. I realise that now. I dismissed it as tittle-tattle, until Mrs. Holmfield came to see me."

"Jealous women can make wild accusations miles from the truth," said Angus. "I know Holmfield's interest in wild flowers is genuine and that he was helping Linda with her collection. His wife's probably the possessive type and resents any interest she doesn't share."

"The bees and the flowers," said Roland with a mocking smile. "That sounds unusually idyllic, coming from you, Angus."

"I thought as you do about Mrs. Holmfield, Angus," said Cynthia, then paused before playing her trump card, making an expressive little gesture with her hands. "But then Peter Holmfield admitted that he and Linda had been having an affair."

"Admitted it?" said Luke harshly.

"Yes. I'm afraid this is all very distressing for you, LG, and so disappointing after all you've done for Linda. I would have tried to keep it from you, but it's gone too far. Either the Holmfields leave or Linda goes. And, quite frankly, it would be a blow to lose the services of

179

the Holmfields, who are both invaluable in their spheres, especially Mrs. Holmfield. I can understand her determination to go if Linda stays here. She's right to protect her marriage. She has David to think of."

"See if Linda's back. If she is, send for her and the Holmfields," said Luke grimly.

"Don't you think it might be wiser to see Linda after you've talked to the Holmfields?" said Cynthia.

"No. If they are making accusations and admissions about Linda, it's only right that she should be present to answer them."

"Does she know of the accusations?" asked Angus.

"No. I was so shocked by Mrs. Holmfield's tale and Peter Holmfield's admission that things had gone so far that I felt I needed time to think it over, and as your grandfather was due here today, I wanted to have his advice before doing anything."

"Quite," said Angus with a sardonic lift to his eyebrows which Cynthia ignored.

"Well, let's get on with it," said Luke sharply. "Nasty business. No good shirking it. Leave it to me, Cynthia. Just see if Linda's back. This is a fine thing to have to cope with as soon as we arrive, I must say."

Linda had just arrived back and came in eagerly a few minutes later, greeting Mr. Ferndale with a smile and turning to Angus with a happy expression which faded as she sensed the cold climate. Before she could ask what the matter was, the Holmfields arrived.

"I'll handle this, Cynthia," said Luke Ferndale harshly. "I don't want a lot of embroidery. I want facts. Now, Mrs. Holmfield, you first. You have made certain accusations to Mrs. Ferndale against Miss Dawley. Kindly repeat them to me, with your grounds for making them."

Linda's bewilderment turned to incredulity as she listened to Enid Holmfield's story, told with cold vindictiveness. "I don't blame my husband," she concluded. "It's that girl, chasing him. Young women have got no decency these days. No respect for marriage. Pretending to be interested in David. Using my son . . ." She stopped as Luke held up his hand.

"That's enough, Mrs. Holmfield. I said facts, not opinions. Your husband, I may remind you, is many years older than Miss Dawley and responsible for his own actions."

"But this is ridiculous," cried Linda. "There's not a word of truth in it. Mrs. Holmfield, you must believe me. You're mistaken. I've taken David out and Peter has joined us sometimes, but we've never met alone by arrangement, and there's never been anything between your husband and me but the most casual friendship and I've . . ."

"I'm not interested in your lies. I've seen with my own eyes. Trying to break up our family. I know your sort."

"Stop this!" thundered Luke. "I said facts, and nothing more. You, Holmfield, what have you to say?"

Peter Holmfield, his face drawn and his eyes tormented, turned to Cynthia appealingly.

"Just tell the truth," said Cynthia quietly. "It will be best for all."

"I'm sorry," he muttered. "My wife has gone too far in her accusations, but I admit I've been foolish. It was all my fault." He avoided Linda's incredulous eyes and stared at his hands helplessly. Nobody could have looked more guilty.

"Peter!" exclaimed Linda.

"I'm sorry. I take full blame."

"How long has this been going on?" asked Angus coldly.

Peter made no reply and his wife answered the question.

"They've been using the beach hut for their love nest these two months or more. I can tell you that."

"It was merely a meeting place," said Holmfield.

"With a key to lock yourselves in?" said his wife.

"With a key so that I could get out the chairs and have them on the verandah. You go too far, Enid."

"I will not have this turning into a squalid argument," said Luke. "You, Holmfield, were meeting Miss Dawley frequently at the beach hut in the evenings, staying there late at night. It's expecting a lot of your wife, to believe that those meetings were platonic, and whether they were or not, it was dishonourable conduct."

"I know he bitterly regrets what's happened," said Cynthia.

"Maybe," snapped Enid Holmfield, "and I don't doubt she led him on. He might have thought of his son, though, if he didn't consider me."

"All right. That's enough. You can go now, both of you," said Luke.

"I've made it clear to Mrs. Ferndale that it's that girl or me. If she stays, I go, and my husband too. I'm not going to stand by and see my marriage wrecked by her," said Enid Holmfield, looking at Linda with the same hatred which she had shown in the nursing home.

"You can leave that to Mr. Ferndale," said Cynthia. "I'll see you later."

"Very well."

After the door had closed behind them, Luke turned to Linda.

"You still deny it, in spite of Holmfield's admission?"

"Yes. I've never met him at the beach hut. I've never been out alone with him except for the odd encounters in the hotel grounds."

"I suppose anybody could get hold of that spare beach hut key without much trouble," said Angus.

"Not unless they asked for it," said

Austin. "It's kept in a drawer of the reception desk which is locked when the girls finish at night."

"Who has the other key?"

"The beach boy."

"Any explanation as to how Peter Holmfield had it, then, Linda?" asked Angus.

"No. I've no idea. It's seldom wanted and I didn't know it wasn't in the drawer with the other spare keys."

Luke Ferndale, who had been standing by the window, hands clasped behind his back, now turned to them and said in a voice which shook with anger:

"I see little point in post-mortems. The man's admitted that he's been carrying on with Linda. He did have the grace to look thoroughly ashamed of himself, as well he might. Linda seems to think she can go on pulling wool over our eyes in spite of the facts and Holmfield's admission. You can tell Mrs. Holmfield that Linda will be returning to England with us. I take it you can dispense with her services straight away, Austin?"

"Yes. Jean can carry on until we get another assistant. No need to upset yourself too much over it, Father. After all, it's not such an uncommon situation."

"Not uncommon to indulge in loose conduct with a married man? It's uncommon in my circle, Austin, I assure you. I may be old-fashioned, but I don't take such conduct lightly. I'm shocked that Linda could behave so dishonourably. I'd never have believed it of her."

"Well, we all make mistakes of judgment some time. After all, you knew nothing about Linda when you took her up with such enthusiasm. A bit of an eye-opener to me, too, perhaps, but then in these days standards are not what they were," said Austin.

If he had deliberately set out to exacerbate his father still more, which he did not, he could not have improved on those remarks. The old man's face was flushed with anger and his voice rose as he said:

"Partly because people like you, who know better, show weak-kneed tolerance instead of denouncing such conduct for what it is, shameful and wicked."

"Well, let's keep the temperature down," said Angus. "No need to get steamed up. And before you start denouncing you might bear in mind what I said at the time: to take an inexperienced girl from a simple, solitary life and throw her into this kind of hot-house existence is inviting her to lose her head."

Luke glared at his grandson, who was sitting on a corner of the table watching the smoke rise from his cigarette, his eyes veiled, wearing that air of studied coolness which always infuriated the old man when his own feelings were running high.

"Linda's not a child. She's twenty-four. Old enough to know right from wrong."

"If a person's not used to drink, they can very soon get intoxicated. It's a heady atmosphere in this sunshine holiday land," said Angus sceptically.

"But Linda had a job of work to do, and your parents were here to give her a family background."

Linda looked round at them helplessly. Austin Ferndale and his wife, Roland, Angus and his grandfather, all discussing her, the prisoner at the bar. She felt stunned by the events which had propelled her so precipitately from the dizzy heights of happiness at the prospect of seeing Angus again to the dark morass which now engulfed her. The old man was hunched like an angry bull. Angus looked calm and collected, and a small smile seemed to hover at his lips as he looked at his father and stepmother and said in the deep, unhurried voice which in some odd way seemed to sharpen the impact of his words:

"So they were, and I'm sure they did it most conscientiously. Still, if you tried for a year to think up a place where it was easy for young people to lose their heads, you wouldn't improve on this hotel in this place. Sunny days, warm nights, romantic scenery, music, a sensuous luxury, the lot. Everything conducive to falling in love."

Linda remembered as he spoke the night of the Viennese dance and afterwards, when he had kissed her too briefly, and she rested her head on her hand feeling as though her heart was being mangled.

"To falling in love with a man who has a wife and a child?" said Luke.

"And," broke in Austin, nettled by that little smile of his son's, "you forget this wasn't a momentary infatuation. One isolated lapse. It was planned. The meetings at the hut, the concealment, it had been going on for weeks."

"It's no good, Angus. You can't make it into anything but thoroughly unprincipled behaviour on both Linda's and Holmfield's part. I wish it were otherwise," said Cynthia.

"Angus is right in one thing," said Luke. "I *was* foolish to give Linda this chance. I realise that now. But I thought she was a decent girl of good principles."

"Such principles come easier when you're old, I guess," said Angus wryly.

At this, Luke banged his fist on the table.

"I've lived by them all my life, and so did Linda's mother. What are principles worth if they won't stand up to temptation? It's only too clear to me where Linda's character stems from. Her father. A man of no moral fibre. Self-indulgent, no sense of responsibility, no consideration for others, living his own Bohemian life at no matter what cost to his wife. I might have known. Linda looks so like her mother that it misled me into thinking she was of the same quality."

And now Linda stood up.

"If you have all finished," she said quietly, "I'd like to say something. My father was a kind and honest man, too

189

sensitive for this world, perhaps. But that is beside the point. It's kind of you, Angus, to try to make excuses for what you believe I've done in spite of my denials, but your grandfather is right. There is no excuse for trying to take a husband from his wife and child. I'm old enough to know that and nothing in my upbringing could have influenced me to think differently. But the truth is, and I know now that you won't believe it, I have not been having a love affair with Peter Holmfield and there has never been anything more between us than the most casual friendship, scarcely that."

"Then why did the man admit it? It's not exactly something to boast about. Why did he plead guilty of most if not all of his wife's accusations if he didn't know that in the face of the evidence it was useless to deny it?" demanded Luke.

"I don't know. I just can't understand it," said Linda helplessly.

"I'd sooner you showed some regret and admitted it, like Holmfield, instead of maintaining this stupid attitude. His wife saw you embracing on the cliffs together, coming away from the beach hut late at night. The man admits it. It's been common gossip, it seems, for weeks past. There's no point in your persisting in this foolish denial," said Luke.

"I can see that, but it's still the truth."

"I'm not going to bandy any more words with you, Linda. This is a bitter disappointment to me. One of the bitterest of my life. I was so happy to have you back, my goddaughter, the child of my very dear friend. I had forgotten your father. You're more his daughter than hers. It's as well to have discovered that sooner than later, perhaps. You may think this a lot of fuss about nothing. I'm not taken in by your high-sounding professions of agreement with me when your actions say the opposite. To you, this is probably a trivial affair which was unluckily found out. But I'll not condone it, nor forget how you've responded to the opportunity I gave you. When we get back to England, I shall give you a sum sufficient to keep you for a few weeks while you look for another job, but I shan't want to see you again. People have disappointed me before, Linda, but I don't believe any disappointment has been as painful to me as this. That's all."

He moved to the door, shuffling a little,

looking suddenly tired and unhappy as he added:

"I shall go and lie down for an hour, Austin. I'll join you all for dinner. That flight's tired me."

Angus, opening the door for his grandfather, said:

"Shall I ask for a drink to be sent to your room? A brandy? You look all in."

"No, I'll just have a quiet nap, boy. Tomorrow, we'll get down to business."

"We thought of having a quiet little family dinner party at Roland's bungalow this evening so that you can be introduced to Angela's daughter. Help you to forget all this unpleasant business, dear," said Cynthia.

Luke nodded but said nothing. As Angus closed the door behind him and came back into the room, he wondered whether he had imagined that there were tears in the old man's eyes.

"Well," said Roland, "I must get back to the club-house. See you all at the bungalow this evening."

"And I'd better see Mrs. Holmfield," said Cynthia. "For the time being, you might as well carry on with your duties,

Linda, and please don't discuss this with anybody. There's been enough gossip. I'll see Mrs. Holmfield in your office, Austin. I want to look up the staff file."

"Right. And I've some cheques to make out. Must say I miss Ruth. Hope to goodness she's better next week. See you later, Angus."

"Righto," said Angus.

When they were alone, Angus turned to Linda with an appraising look which gave her no comfort.

"I've never seen the old man so upset. You fool, Linda. You played right into their hands. The one thing the old man would never put up with, and I don't blame him."

"Is it impossible for *you* to believe me when I say I'm innocent of this? We're friends, after all."

"I thought so. And a bit more. But your letters have been very impersonal. Personal affairs in another quarter a bit too intimate to mention, perhaps."

She winced at the irony in his voice. Suddenly, with an impatient gesture, he flung open the windows and went out to the balcony as though stifled, and stood there, gazing down at the fountains in the courtyard. It was growing dark and she watched his dark silhouette against a sky which was showing the first pale stars. She still felt half-dazed, as though she would wake up soon and discover that it had been a nightmare and that Angus was due to arrive. Huddled in the armchair in the darkening room, she could think of nothing more to say to refute this business, but when after a few minutes he came back into the room, she made another effort.

"You know me better than the others, Angus. Surely you can believe me."

"I might, except for two things. I wouldn't put it past my stepmother and Roland to make things look bad for you if they could do it without risk of being found out, but no inducement they could have held out to Mrs. Holmfield to slander you would have brought that hatred for you into being. That woman wasn't acting, Linda. She was absolutely convinced that you were having an affair with her husband. I was watching her closely. Jealousy like that isn't pleasant to watch, and couldn't be feigned. And the facts and details she described were pretty conclusive, I must say."

"I've given her no cause to hate me, but I know she does. And the other thing?"

"Holmfield. I watched him closely, too. He hated giving you away. I worked a good deal with him when I was last here. I didn't get the impression that he was a man who could be bought, and certainly not low enough to incriminate an innocent girl for any financial reward."

"No. The idea's preposterous. Peter's kind and decent. I just can't understand his attitude over this. And why should you think Mrs. Ferndale would want to damage me? She's always been pleasant, if not very friendly, since I've been here."

"Well, it's all beside the point now, but my stepmother and her son love money. My father was the ladder to get to it. They don't want another contender for my grandfather's money. If they could have engineered some way of discrediting you in the old man's eyes, they'd have done so. But you've done it for them."

"It's horrible. I can't believe it. I'm no threat to them."

"Not now. You were. Grandfather made no secret of his intention to adopt you. My stepmother has done a good deal of hatchet work in the past between my grandfather and me. She'd be more than willing to apply the same treatment to you. However, you've saved her the trouble. With all the comings and goings here, you had to fall for a married man with a child. And you didn't waste much time, it seems. It must have started as soon as I was off the scene."

"How can you believe that? I know the circumstances look bad. I can't prove anything. But do you think I'm that kind of person? You've known me for years, after all."

"I knew you as a child. I've not seen much of you as an adult."

"But when you were here in June. We were so close. I felt you knew me and understood me so well. And yet you think I could do this."

"When we were together," he said slowly, "I realised that you were waking up after a solitary and in some ways repressed life. That's what this place, not unnaturally, had done to you. You'd come to life, were aware of yourself as a woman in a way you hadn't been aware when I saw you at Hartfield. In the garden after the dance that night—we both knew it. Holmfield was able to take it on from there, I suppose, and you were too inexperienced, too intoxicated by all this to be able to put the brake on."

Her cheeks flushed as she met his eyes. But I was in love with you, she wanted to cry, and realised how little that would help now. It would only make her seem more fickle and unstable. She was caught in a trap, and the injustice of it made her angry.

"I'm tired of being put in other people's frames for me. Your grandfather saw me in terms of the past, as my mother might have been at my age. To him, I was my mother back from the grave. To you, I was a green child, especially susceptible to men because I'd lived a simple, solitary life for so long, liable from the start to get into man trouble. To your stepmother, apparently, I was merely a threat to their future inheritance. Nobody," she concluded passionately, "accepted me as an individual in my own right, was interested in getting to know me as a person. You all had preconceived ideas. And yours is more insulting than any, implying that I'm too silly and irresponsible to be able to resist any man who lifts a finger to me. That nobody goes off the rails more easily than a repressed person when set free, a late-starter. Hasn't that been at the back of your head all along?"

"Not exactly. But what's happened doesn't make that picture look so wrong, does it? Of course I don't accept Mrs. Holmfield's opinion of you, nor my step-mother's delicate underlining of it. I guess you fell in love in circumstances that were all too favourable, and simply lost your head. Holmfield was right to take the blame. He's much older than you in years and experience, and had no right to lead you into this mess. But where did you think such an infatuation could end?"

"There was no infatuation," cried Linda.

"Well I could use other terms, but I won't," he said coldly. "I've had enough. I'd looked forward to a different reunion, but we live and learn. I wish you'd been more honest about it. To be deeply in love with someone and be swept off your feet by it is understandable, but trying to deny it merely suggests that you hope I'll be able to reinstate you with the old man. You can put that hope aside."

"I have no wish to be reinstated with any

of the Ferndales. My father was right. I should have kept away from them."

"I never wanted to be involved in this, believe me. The family has always spelt trouble for me. But you can scarcely blame this on to them. For myself, I wish I'd followed my own instincts in the first place, and kept out of it all. Right now, however, I've got a battle on my hands over the re-organisation of the hotel, and to have started off with this grubby business hasn't exactly helped to put me in good fettle. I'll see what a drink and a bath will do. I advise you to start thinking of the future. There won't be any reprieve from the old man."

He nodded coolly and left her. And even then, she could hardly believe it.

16

Night flight

WHEN she had collected herself a little, Linda's first thought was to go to Peter and demand an explanation, but the accounts office would be closed by now and she could not go to his bungalow and face his wife, who would assuredly not admit her. Ruth, sick with severe gastritis, could not be bothered with anything just now. There was nobody she felt able to turn to.

Seized with a sudden desire to get right away from the hotel, she went out and walked blindly across the golf course, stumbling in the dark, trying to marshal her thoughts. Burning with the humiliation forced on her that afternoon, tried by a court of Ferndales like a prisoner and dismissed like a dishonest servant by the old man, the one predominant thought that emerged from her walk was a fierce determination not to accept a penny more from

Mr. Ferndale and never again to have any dealings with the family. Her father's warning came back to her. If you accept gifts, you lose your independence which is worth more than any gift. Well, she had accepted Luke Ferndale's generosity, had opened her arms to a new life, and this was where it had got her. And beneath it all, more wounding than anything, the realisation that the love which had sprung up between her and Angus, fragile and barely acknowledged, had been cut off so harshly, for it had been a cold stranger she had just parted with. And for the humiliating picture of her that he had painted, she could never forgive him.

Forcing her mind back to practical matters, she tried to reckon whether she had enough money to pay for her air-ticket back to England, for that was where now she longed to be. She had spent little of her salary here, for everything she could want had been provided by the hotel, and she had about a hundred pounds in her bank account. But even travelling economy class, it would leave her with next to nothing at the other end.

Afterwards, looking back, it seemed that

the most remarkable thing on that remarkable day was the solution to her problem which met her as soon as she set foot in the reception hall on her return to the hotel.

"Ah, Miss Dawley, my last hope!" exclaimed Captain Lock, as he came up to her looking worried.

"What's the matter?"

"Everything," he groaned. "Come over here and give me your advice, because I'm at my wits' end." He led her to a quiet couch along the wall. "I'm recalled to my unit. An emergency. Due back tomorrow. I shall have to fly to New York instead of London tonight. I suppose it's too much to hope that there's anybody flying back to London tonight who could take my kids along with them? I'm trying to contact my wife's parents to get them to meet the plane, so far without luck. They don't answer the telephone, but I'll keep trying. Meanwhile, what am I going to do with Sandra and John? The air hostesses are very good, I know, but the little one's only four, and John's as mischievous as a monkey. And what's going to happen to them at London Airport if I can't contact my wife's people?"

202

"Where do they live?"

"At Richmond, near London. I was going to take them straight there tomorrow morning, spend the day there and fly back to New York tomorrow night."

"Hold on. I'll find out if anybody else is going on this evening's flight to London."

She came back in a few minutes.

"No luck. You're the only passengers from here."

"Is there anyone here who'd do the job for me if I paid them? Anybody who'd like a look at London? My ticket's going free, and they could use my return to New York and step off here instead."

It was as simple as that. Providence, which had hurled thunderbolts at her that afternoon, now held out a helping hand.

"I'm going back to England," she said. "I was planning to go in a few days' time. I'll take the children tonight, Captain Lock, if you'll trust them with me, and I'll deliver them at Richmond if you can't get in touch with their grandparents."

"Oh, my guardian angel! But . . . at such short notice? Can you?"

"Yes. I'm leaving the hotel. I was only a temporary employee, you know, and my

203

time's up. I hadn't bought my air-ticket, and I shall be glad to take yours. I feel I should pay something for it, though. Say, half?"

"My dear Miss Dawley, I shall insist on paying all your expenses and a wage for the job. You'll earn it, believe me."

"No. Just the ticket, then."

In a few minutes their plans were made and Linda left him to go and pack. She had little time, but the urge to escape from this place and the Ferndale family was now so great that she could not get away quickly enough. As she hurried across the hall, she saw them emerge from a lift, but the hall was crowded with people going in to dinner and they did not see her. She watched them cross to the entrance, Mrs. Ferndale and the old man leading, Angus and his father behind. The doorman saluted them and they vanished into the night. And that, she thought, was the last she would ever see of the Ferndales. But however far she ran, she knew it would not be easy to forget Angus.

In her room, she packed her few private possessions and any clothes she had bought herself. Those which Mrs. Ferndale had bought for her, she left. Then she wrote a letter to old Mr. Ferndale. She had little time to choose her words and could only write as she felt.

Dear Mr. Ferndale,

I have a chance of returning to London on the night flight, escorting two young children whose father at the last minute is unable to accompany them to their grandparents' home. I am taking this opportunity of leaving as you made it quite clear this afternoon that the sooner you were relieved of my presence, the better, and I, too, cannot escape quickly enough from a situation that is so painful and humiliating.

I am taking only what belongs to me and the money saved from my salary since I've been here.

I know that what you did for me, you meant most kindly and for that I thank you. I repeat that I am completely innocent of the charges made against me this afternoon, but I admit that appearances were against me. Perhaps it's unreasonable of me to have expected more trust in my denials, but I did.

I am sorry that things have turned out

like this, but the fault is not mine. Your remarks about my father, however, confirm the wisdom of this parting of the ways. I don't belong to the Ferndales, and never could now, and the link you tried to forge has only damaged us both. My father was above all a gentle man and I have never been conditioned to harshness such as I experienced this afternoon. I hope I never shall again.

Yours sincerely,
Linda Dawley

She would have liked to write to Ruth, but had no time. She left the letter in Mr. Ferndale's pigeon-hole in the hall, cashed a cheque with the hotel cashier for the money in her account, and found Captain Lock and the two children waiting for her in the hall. His flight back to New York left soon after hers, and she was glad that he would be able to see them off.

As the taxi moved away from the noisy, crowded hotel down the palm-lined drive, she still felt in the grip of a strange un-reality. The lights in Roland's bungalow were shining out as they passed, then there was only the twisting lane between the hibiscus hedges. It was a warm night with stars glittering in a black velvet sky.

"Guess this is a romantic sort of place," said Captain Lock.

"Very."

"Have you enjoyed being here?"

"Yes. But I'm homesick now."

"For London?"

"No. The English countryside. And Cornwall."

"Cornwall? That's where my wife spent her childhood. She took me back there once. Your home there?"

As they talked about Cornwall, Linda felt a hunger for the wild solitude she had known so well. Then, it had sometimes seemed too solitary, but now it seemed like a stern old friend offering her refuge.

Sandra was half asleep against her father, John, wide-eyed and silent, looked a little scared and Linda put an arm round his shoulder as they talked.

"Roots. It must be good to have roots in a place," said Captain Lock. "That's something a soldier never has. Well, here we are. I'll just get these tickets sorted out. You wait here with Miss Dawley, kids."

Having the children to look after was a

blessing, she found, for it left her no time to brood over her own troubles. Sandra was too sleepy to know much about what was going on, but John's lips trembled when his father said goodbye.

"Don't worry about them, Captain Lock. I'll take good care of them, and I'll send a cable to the address you've given me just as soon as I've left them with their grandparents," said Linda.

"You help Miss Dawley all you can, son. I'll be over on my next leave. And thanks again, Miss Dawley," he said, pressing her hand. "You've been swell. Don't know what I'd have done if you hadn't come to our rescue."

The goodbyes over, Linda found herself walking across the tarmac to the waiting aeroplane, a child holding each hand. They waved from the top of the steps, and then the air hostess took them over. The aeroplane was already half full, for it had come from New York. Almost as soon as they were settled, the aeroplane was moving along the runway, and Linda was too occupied with the children even to see the lights of Bermuda dwindle behind them.

That morning, she had been awaiting

Angus with joy and an eager impatience, she had an interesting job, a luxurious background, congenial companions at work. Twelve hours later, she had lost it all, including her reputation, and was on her way back to England with no job, no home, no relatives to turn to and a little less than one hundred pounds behind her. These facts, however, she pushed to the back of her mind while she concentrated on reassuring John, whose world, too, had crumbled, and who was only seven years old.

17

Dead yesterday

ENGLAND that October was enjoying an Indian summer, and during her first week at the little inn near the north coast of Cornwall, the sun shone out of a clear blue sky and a quiet calm reigned over all. If the temperature seemed cool by comparison with Bermuda, the freshness of the air with its autumnal nip acted like a tonic on Linda so that the unhappy inertia that had followed the numbness of shock now gave way to more positive thinking.

The village where she was staying was only a few miles from the cottage that had been her home, and she borrowed a bicycle and returned there one day. It looked smaller than she expected and the garden was overgrown. A farmworker lived there now, she was told, but the only indication of life was a line of washing. It would be easy to let nostalgia persuade her that the life she had led there had been idyllic, but the truth was that it had been a hard, lonely life, tempered by the solace of nature and her father's affection. But it had never hurt her as life with the Ferndales had hurt her. Her horizons had widened, though, since her father's death and the clock could not be put back. She was not the same person as the girl who had lived in this remote corner of the country, but coming back to it had in some way helped her to get her balance again.

She left her bicycle propped against a tree near the cottage and walked out to the cliff and along to a combe running down to the sea which was well known to her. Here, sheltered from the wind, the first primroses were to be found, and botanically it had been her father's favourite hunting ground. A small stream ran down it, bordered by reeds and long grass of a richer green than any she had seen abroad. She scrambled down to a rocky outcrop near the stream, and sat there in the sun, her shoes wet with the dew which sparkled on the grass around her. Below, a gentle sea washed the rocky little beach with waves scarcely strong enough to turn over. Save for an occasional gull, her solitude was complete. At the top of the combe, against the skyline, a small group of hawthorn trees stood, leaning away from the south-west, their branches shaped in a slanting line as though a giant's knife had sliced their tops off, reminding her of the gales which blew with such frightening force on this coast, hard to imagine in these days of halcyon calm.

A red admiral butterfly arrived to sun itself on a rock near by. Watching it, she thought of the sophisticated life and almost feverish activity of the hotel in Bermuda. The contrast could not have been greater. Now, she had time to think, with no distractions, and as she sat there, she looked back over the months since she had ventured into the orbit of the Ferndales, and took stock. She remembered the patronage that had given her such an inferiority complex in those early days; the way old Mr. Ferndale had taken possession of her, to groom her to be a credit to him; the polite but always cool treatment she had received from his son and his wife and Roland, excluding her from any family gatherings, treating her as just another employee; the conversation she had overheard between Angus and his aunt, and his subsequent attitude, reducing her to the stature of a child in need of protection; and, burning still in her heart, the humiliation of that court-martial when all their attitudes had crystallised into one ruthless condemnation which took no account of her denials, followed by a sentence of dismissal, with disgrace. Now that she could see the picture as a whole, she was angry with herself for the facile way in which she had allowed herself to be taken over. The arrogance of wealth. She remembered her father using those words about Luke Ferndale. It applied to the whole family. An arrogance, a dictatorship. Her father had warned her, but she had had to learn about it the hard way. And perhaps it was against Angus that her anger burned most fiercely because from him the hurt went deepest.

Her father was right. Independence mattered more than anything, and she would never forget that again. People let you down. The Ferndales, Peter, and even Ruth, who had sent no reply to the letter she had written as soon as she arrived in Cornwall explaining what had happened and hoping that they could keep their friendship alive through letters. It would have meant much to her to have received some assurance of trust from somebody. In future, she would rely on herself, and it was this determination that inclined her to search for some way of earning a living on her own, free of employers.

And so, sitting there on the slope of the combe, she made her summing up and began to think about the future, resolutely blotting out the dark face of Angus which had been haunting her.

As the sunny days of October slipped away, her resolution strengthened. She went for long solitary walks along the cliffs or along the firm sands with the boom of the waves and the hiss of the surf beside her. And always the message was the same. Her father's way was best.

At the end of the month, her mind clear and determined, she approached the innkeeper about the chalet standing closed and deserted in the field behind.

"We let it in the summer to holiday-makers," he said.

"Would you rent it to me for the winter?"

He looked surprised. He was a burly, good-natured man, with a slow, deliberate way of speaking.

"Well, m'dear, it's not exactly a cosy winter home. A bit bleak and lonely for a young woman like you."

"I want to do some writing," she said, "and it would tide me over until I see if I can make a go of it."

"Ah, one of they authors," he observed, as though that explained such lunacy. "Well, it's all right by me. Glad to get a pound a week for it, if that's what you want. The wife could take in what food you need, but you'd better have a good look at the place in the morning. I've never reckoned on it being suitable for winter accommodation."

"I'll do that."

In bed that night, she made her plans. If the chalet was at all habitable, she would see if she could earn enough money to keep herself by using the only experience she had—apart from that of hotel receptionist which she had no wish to use again—that of typist and quasi-literary assistant to her father. She had typed all that he had written, corrected his proofs when his eyes began to fail, and latterly had collaborated with him in a small way. She would like to try her skill now at country articles and a children's book, the idea for which had come into her mind after her short contact with the Lock children. She would advertise, too, for manuscripts to type. She still had the old portable typewriter which had been her father's, and her overheads would be small. She had enough money, she reckoned, to keep herself for six months, even if she earned nothing, provided the chalet was a possible habitation.

Immediately after breakfast the next morning, she took the key from the innkeeper and walked across the grass to have a look at it. The wooden structure was painted green. It had a verandah, and inside she found a good-sized bed-sitting-room, two small bedrooms, a kitchen, and in what was not much more than a lean-to at the back there had been fashioned a primitive bathroom. There was a calor gas cooker in the kitchen and an oil stove in the bed-sitting-room. The bare bedsteads and plain furniture made it look bleak, but the rooms were light, the place was clean, and, with a little rearranging, she thought that she could make it reasonably comfortable. Heating would be the difficulty, but if she bought another oil stove to supplement the existing one, it should be all right.

She agreed to take it, and a second oil-stove was provided by Mrs. Fettal, the innkeeper's wife, who also hung some curtains, provided coverlets and cushions which transformed the unwanted beds into couches, and found a comfortable chair and a sturdy table for the typewriter. If the atmosphere within still remained a little stark, the view from the sitting-room window across the meadow to the combe which ran down to the sea offered good compensation, and Linda moved in at the beginning of November.

"I'll be surprised if you see the winter out there, m'dear," said Jim Fettal, "but you can have it as long as you want it, up until Easter. It seems a right quiet life for a young woman, though, writer or not, and I doubt you'll stick it out for long, once the winter really sets in," with which gloomy prognostication he continued polishing the glasses behind the bar.

But Linda did stick it out and found a certain peace of mind there, chiefly because she found writing an occupation which could absorb her to the exclusion of all else. The solitude which might have weighed on her during the dark days of winter was ameliorated by the kindness of the Fettals, with whom she spent many evenings. Journalism earned her a few pounds, and her father's publishers expressed interest in the children's book which she outlined to them, and she undertook to submit the finished typescript to them in the spring. She was not successful, however, in attracting any typing through an advertisement which she had placed in a newspaper covering the south-west, and early in January she tried one in a national literary paper. This, too, produced no work but a consequence of a different nature.

She was working on her book one grey, windy afternoon early in February when there was a knock at the door. She opened it, expecting to see Mrs. Fettal with some eggs, but it was Angus Ferndale who stood there.

"Hullo," he said. "Can I come in?"

He was already in, and Linda closed the door and stood with her back to it, as though at bay.

"So this is where you've hidden yourself," he went on, looking around. "I've been trying to find you for months. What on earth made you do that disappearing act?"

"I should have thought it was obvious. How did you find out where I was?"

"Aunt Harriet spotted your advertisement in the literary monthly she takes in. Funny thing is, I came down here in December and had a look round. Went to your old home, made a few enquiries, but nobody seemed to have heard of you."

"Why did you want to see me? I thought our last meeting was pretty final."

"Don't stand there looking at me as though I'm a dangerous animal. We received a letter from Peter Holmfield in December. Here it is. May I sit down while you read it?" he asked wryly.

She indicated the divan as she took the letter from him. It covered sheets of flimsy paper, and turning her back on him she sat

219

down at her work-table to read it. It was dated the fourth of December.

Dear Mr. Ferndale,

I have a confession to make which I am afraid will shock and anger you, but I hope no lasting damage has been done and that this will set the record right.

When I admitted to that affair with Linda Dawley I was lying. I did so to protect the woman I had loved for the past year and more. Ruth Elsted, your son's secretary. It was made easy for me because Mrs. Ferndale told me that she would make light of it to you and that you were always very indulgent towards Linda and would merely view it as a foolish escapade. She said that Linda was only at the hotel temporarily anyway, and that since my wife was convinced of Linda's guilt, the best way out for all was for Linda to have her stay curtailed. It seemed such an easy solution to a deplorable situation, and if I had denied it, I was afraid my wife would have got on to Ruth, and that I could not have borne.

Ruth was delicate, and at the time you may remember was ill. Discovery would have lost her her job and ruined our happiness. Linda, I thought, would not lose much. When I saw your reaction, and Linda disappeared the next day, I realised that Mrs. Ferndale's prediction had proved wrong and when Linda wrote to Ruth, I learned from her letter the harm that had been done and knew that I would have to put it right some time. But I had only one thought in all this— to protect Ruth. If it had not been for my son, I would have taken Ruth away long ago.

I don't know whether you have heard, but Ruth died last week after two months in hospital. No harm can come to her now. I deeply regret having hurt Linda, who heaven knows had done nothing to deserve it. She had been very kind to my son and I liked her. But it would be hypocritical to say that I wish I had not done it, since to protect Ruth I would do it again. I think in our hearts, Ruth and I both knew our happiness had only a brief time to run. That is why we took risks. I shall never regret it.

I kept Linda's letter from Ruth and she never knew what had happened. I merely said that Linda had returned home with you. Ruth was too ill to query anything. I was with her when she died, very peacefully.

I wanted to write all this to Linda, but I stupidly burnt her letter before noting the address, which I believe was only a temporary one, anyway. I only remember that it was in Cornwall. However, you will no doubt know her whereabouts, and I should be grateful if you would tell her how sorry I am that I had to make her the scapegoat. But since she knew Ruth and was fond of her, too, I think perhaps she will find it in her heart to forgive me.

I have not told Mrs. Ferndale about this, as my wife and I are leaving here at the end of the month to go to a hotel in the Bahamas. May I ask you not to inform her until we have gone? I would rather Ruth's name was not bandied about in my presence, and I don't want my wife ever to know. I have no right to ask this, of course, but I do. When we have gone, it will not matter.

I have no doubt you will think my conduct dishonourable. I can't excuse it.

My love for Ruth was stronger than honour or anything else. That is all. If this seems a very bald statement of facts, it is because I find it too painful to write more.

Yours sincerely,
Peter Holmfield

Linda put the letter down, remembering the words Ruth had quoted to her that day when they had seen the blue bird in the hibiscus hedge. "Unborn tomorrow and dead yesterday, why fret about them if today be sweet!" That bird of time had indeed but a little way to fly, and Ruth had known it.

"Poor Ruth," said Linda softly.

"Grandfather's all burned up about it. What can I say, Linda? Only that we're sorry."

"Did your grandfather wait until Peter and his family had gone before writing to your stepmother?"

"Yes."

"I'm glad."

"He wants you to come back to Hartfield, Linda. He wants to make amends. Not that he could be blamed for thinking Holmfield spoke the truth."

"Instead of me," said Linda quietly.

Angus was leaning forward, his hands on his knees, watching her through narrowed eyes, sensing the change in her.

"Well, what about it? Coming back to Hartfield," he said.

"Did you really think, after all that was said of me that day, and of my father, that you had only to say that it was a mistake to have me running happily back to the shelter of Hartfield?"

"The old man's very upset about it. He may have been harsh, but he has a keen sense of justice, and he has only one idea now, to remedy the injustice done to you. As soon as he got that letter, he sent me out, scouring the Cornish countryside. I thought you might have come back to your old haunts. He's been in a regular pother ever since, and when Aunt Harriet spotted your address in that paper, he couldn't wait to get me down here to fetch you home, as he put it."

"To fetch me home. A typical Ferndale attitude. I am not a child to be taken here and there, spoilt, bullied, fetched home.

224

When will you get that into your head? I'm adult, Angus. Nearly twenty-five. Capable of looking after myself. It was the biggest mistake of my life when I accepted your grandfather's patronage. Perhaps it was as well that Peter Holmfield did what he did, since it showed me your family in its true colours and made me see how foolish I'd been ever to give up my freedom and independence. No, Angus, I shall never come back to Hartfield. I bear your grandfather no grudge. I'll write him a note, so that he needn't feel guilty or troubled about it. But my path isn't going to cross the Ferndales' again."

"You can't forgive the damage to your pride, can you? Your father was the same, I believe. And, like him, you're contracting out, burying yourself in this outlandish place, nursing your grievance against the world."

"Not at all. I'm very contented here. I intend to earn my living by writing if I can. This place serves very well as a starting point. It's peaceful, quiet, and cheap. And I've received nothing but kindness since I've come here, which is more than I can say of my stay in Bermuda."

"You've changed." He leaned back against the wall and took out a cigarette. "May I?"

"I can't stop you."

"Claws. I'm sorry I hurt you so much, Linda. Don't you think you're cutting off your nose now to spite your face, though?"

"There you go again. Talking down to me like a child. You're insufferable. Your arrogance. The Ferndale arrogance. My father found it intolerable, and so do I. When I heard you talking to your aunt Harriet that night—I should have known then. I think I did . . . Never mind. Let me make this clear before you go. I'm making a new life for myself. A free life, an independent life. It doesn't contain the Ferndales and never will. Not any of them. Is that clear?"

"A challenge?" he asked, his black eyes gleaming.

"No challenge. A statement of fact. Now, out of politeness to an old man, I'll write a note to your grandfather. When I've finished it, I'll be obliged if you'll go."

"You really mean that?" he asked, his eyebrows raised as though he found the idea faintly amusing as well as incredible.

Something in his expression brought the colour to her cheeks and she turned away, furious.

"Yes, I do mean it," she said curtly, and took out a sheet of notepaper from her drawer. It was only with an effort that she was able to stop her hand from trembling so that she could write.

Dear Mr. Ferndale,

Angus has shown me Peter Holmfield's letter and I am naturally glad to have my name cleared.

Please do not worry about it any more. It's in the past now. Ruth Elsted was my friend and I am very unhappy at Peter's news. She was a kind, gentle person, who had suffered ill health for most of her life and I'm glad that Peter protected her to the end, not only for Ruth's sake. That last meeting with you and your family opened my eyes to many things, among them the realisation that Dawleys and Ferndales do not mix happily. Shall we say they are just incompatible? Which is why I must refuse your invitation to Hartfield.

For your kindness in the past, thank

you. The rest I shall forget, so there need be no hard feelings and regrets. But this is goodbye.

Yours sincerely,
Linda

She handed it to Angus, saying:

"Read it, because the message is the same for you."

He read it, a wry expression on his face, and observed as he folded it and put it in the inner pocket of his overcoat:

"I wouldn't say it could be exactly the same for me, would you?"

"In what respect do you think it should differ?"

"In one sense I'd say we do mix happily. And it's no use saying there are no hard feelings and you'll forget, when you're flaming mad with me and obviously intend to remember me with a permanent grudge."

"I thought you were my friend. But the truth was that you were only patronising me, as your grandfather did. Giving the simpleton up from the country a good time, warning her not to read too much into it because you felt it all too likely that she would fall in love with you."

"How presumptuous of me," he said wickedly, and she wanted to strike him.

"In your eyes I was a repressed, silly creature likely to fling herself at any man, married or not. You rather enjoyed playing with me for a few weeks, exercising your charm. But your profession of friendship meant so little that a man, almost a stranger to you, only had to imply that I'd been having an affair with him and you believed him in spite of my denials. You were ready to believe I was a liar, a weakling, a man-chaser. And even then, you were more annoyed because I'd played into your step-mother's hands than concerned about me. I was a tool you could use against her and I'd rendered myself ineffective. I find you all equally objectionable."

"And you talk about arrogance! I find you objectionable at this moment, my girl. Your pride insists on distorting every-thing. That's what comes of burying your-self down here with nothing to keep you from brooding over it all. Why did you run off like that, without a word to me?"

"I'd had enough words to know that I was condemned, with no appeal."

"A mistake was made. I've said I'm sorry. The old man's been saying it for weeks past. What more do you want?"

"I don't know why you go on, Angus," said Linda calmly, glad that at last she had made him angry. "You came to ask me to return to Hartfield. I've refused, and I have every right to, since this is a free country. It's been interesting meeting the Ferndales again, and learning that my father was right about them. The experience has been salutary. Now I must ask you to go, because I've a lot of work on hand."

"Gladly," said Angus coldly. "Until you get that outsize chip off your shoulder, it's useless talking to you."

"What sort of a tame puppy do you think I am, to expect me to wag my tail and come back and ask for more?"

"Answer me one thing truthfully. Who did the most damage? My grandfather or me?"

"On balance, you."

"I see," he said slowly.

"But don't think it matters any more," she said quickly. "I'm quite cured, and very happy in my new life, with no hankerings to take up with the Ferndales ever again."

He took her by the shoulders then and she tried to meet his eyes steadily. There was a long silence, then he said, "Liar," and walked to the door. At the threshold he turned and looked round the room before bringing his eyes back to her.

"If and when you're ready to come out of your bolt-hole, we'll fight it out," he said, and then he was gone.

Linda stood staring at the closed door for a few moments, then sat down at the table and willed herself not to cry. He had badly dented her new-found peace, but she could and would drive him out again.

He had left Peter's letter with her, and she picked it up and read it again, her heart aching for Ruth. She supposed old Mr. Ferndale would condemn Ruth just as he had condemned her, but Linda could only think of the sad waste and frustration of it all. Love came unbidden, not to conventional order, and when it could not be fulfilled, it was a matter for compassion. But compassion was something that was missing from the Ferndale character.

18

Change of tide

AFTER Angus's visit, Linda threw herself into her work with more determination than ever, and finished her book at the beginning of March. In an odd way, it had helped to ease the soreness in her heart, this simple family tale of the impact of two children on their grandparents' lives. Perhaps it was a happy omen that she had written the last sentence on her twenty-fifth birthday and had received that morning a birthday card from Sandra and John Lock, who had given her the idea for the book. She smiled as she read the large uneven printing of good wishes on the back of the card. She had kept up an intermittent correspondence with the children ever since sending John a card and a book on his eighth birthday, which had fallen a week after their arrival in England, a fact made known to her by John during that endless night flight back.

Sandra had added some kisses. She propped the card up on the wooden shelf above the divan, touched that John had remembered in their exchange about birthdays that hers was the first of March. It was, she thought, the only recognition of her birthday, but later in the day Mrs. Fettal brought over a small flat parcel. Linda put it aside while they chatted. It was Angus's writing on the parcel and she wanted to be alone when she opened it.

"I've just finished my book, Mrs. Fettal, and almost wish I hadn't. I shall miss my characters."

"Well, that's worked out fine. Now you'll be able to get out more, with spring on the doorstep. You're looking a little pale, dear. I never thought you'd stay the winter, you know. Nor did Jim. Didn't seem right somehow, you so young, and all on your own. But we've been glad to have you, and we'll be right sorry to lose you. I'd turn down the holiday bookings if we could afford to, but . . ."

"Of course you can't afford to lose the income. I know that, Mrs. Fettal. I'm grateful to you both for letting me have the chalet so cheaply all the winter. I must start looking round for other quarters now that I've finished my book. I can stay until Easter, can't I?"

"Yes. And if you care to move across to the inn just for Easter, you could have the chalet again until Whitsun. After that, it's fully booked. You can have our spare room over Easter, though, and welcome."

"Thank you, Mrs. Fettal. You've both been so kind. I haven't thought where I'll go yet, but your offer will give me more time to look around."

When she was alone, Linda opened the parcel. It contained a book of the complete works of her favourite modern poet. On the flyleaf was written: Linda, from Angus, and the date. Inside was a short note.

Dear Linda,

This is going to give you a splendid opportunity for a comeback which you may find hard to resist. I hope you will resist it, though, and not return the book, or else I shall think you really did mean those things you said!

I can't think that your birthday will be exactly festive, presuming you still to be in your nun's retreat, but may I send my best wishes? I do, anyway.

Yours,
Angus

It was cleverly worded to make it difficult for her to return it, but she had only to recall that last scene in the hotel to have her resolution stiffened and her amazement at his arrogance increased. Every word he had said on that occasion was as clear in her mind as though he had just spoken it. And afterwards he had gone out with the others to dine at the bungalow, leaving her alone at a time when she so desperately needed a little kindness. Now, after the insults and the trial and the sentence of dismissal, a present and the acknowledgment that it was all a mistake should wipe it all out, as though it had never happened.

She repacked the book and posted it back to him, firm in the conviction that that was the end of her contact with the Ferndales.

Resolutely thrusting Angus from her mind, she spent the next few weeks searching in the vicinity for suitable accommodation for the next stage in her independent life. To her delight, the publishers approved of her book and offered her a contract, intimating that they would like more books of a similar type. The advance they paid her and the odd amounts she was now earning from journalism were enough to see her over the next six months if she could find somewhere cheap to live.

She was studying the figures of her budget on a Saturday morning at the end of March when there was a knock at the door. To her amazement, it was Harriet Ferndale who stood there.

"Good morning, Linda," she said. "May I come in?"

She looked older, Linda thought as she invited her to take a seat. Loosening her coat and putting her bag and gloves on the divan beside her, Harriet met Linda's enquiring gaze with a serious, appraising look before saying abruptly:

"You're surprised to see me. Well, I won't beat about the bush. Father had a stroke three weeks ago. He's still quite ill, and he's fretting about you. It's become an obsession with him. I've come to ask you to return to Hartfield, even if only for a short time, to reassure him."

There was a pause, then Linda said quietly:

"I'm so sorry. He seemed such a strong, vital person that it's hard to realise."

"Well, he's seventy-nine, after all. And he's always driven himself hard. It's amazing that he survived the stroke. He's not out of the wood yet. One leg is paralysed, and I doubt whether he'll walk again. And there's always the danger of another stroke. He's not a patient invalid, but he'd do better if he'd stop worrying about you."

"Of course I'll come."

"Thank you. Angus said he didn't think you would, but I thought differently."

"Where are you staying now?"

"At a hotel in Bude. Angus drove me down yesterday. We'd like to drive back tomorrow. Could you manage that?"

"Yes. How long do you think I should stay?"

"He'll want you to come back permanently."

"I can't promise that."

"I don't blame you, after what happened. But things are rather different now. He's a very sick man. He's living a lot in the past, and I think I ought to tell you a bit about that. I don't know it all, of course. But it may help you to understand him better. Do you mind if I smoke?"

"Of course not. Hold on and I'll make you some coffee. You look tired, Miss Ferndale. You must have had a very worrying time."

"Yes. It's been a shock. Like seeing an old oak tree struck by lightning."

Pouring out the coffee, Linda was again aware of Harriet Ferndale's close scrutiny.

"Sugar?"

"No, thank you. A lot's happened since I saw you last, Linda, hasn't it? You've learned more of the world, I guess."

"Yes."

"Not all bad, I hope?"

"All experience, anyhow. And salutary, no doubt."

"You've grown up. Well, that's a painful process, but you may find it easier to forgive my father's harshness in the light of what I've got to say. You don't have to tell me what he was like to you in Bermuda. I know more about his harshness and his dictatorial ways than anyone alive, perhaps. But you must try to realise, my dear, that basically his is a simple nature. He's not in the least sophisticated. A puritan, a man of fixed principles which he would stand by at no matter what cost to himself and others. What you did, what he thought you did, was perhaps to him the most unforgivable thing that could have happened because it's what he resisted all his life, and he paid a heavy price for his virtue. You see, he was deeply in love with your mother. I've only learned about it gradually over the years, and indirectly. As you can imagine, my father never confided in anybody. But since his illness, he's let things fall and filled in some facts. He met your mother when she was twenty and fell in love with her then. He was twelve years older than she was, and already married, with one child and a second, that was me, on the way. His code would never allow him to speak of it, but there's no doubt that your mother knew, and returned his love. She didn't marry your father until she was nearly forty, and then because she wanted a child before it was too late. My mother died suddenly just a few months after their marriage, and so my father gained his freedom just too late."

"And that is why he always resented my father, I suppose."

"Yes. And he despised failures and thought your mother deserved better. He would have given her the earth, I do believe."

"I remember him standing by her grave after the funeral, all alone. I didn't think much about it at the time, but the picture always stayed with me. He looked so sad and lonely."

"Yes. I'm a realist myself, and not given to romance, but in my father's case it's true to say that he loved your mother from the time he met her, and still does. I'm quite sure no word passed between them that he would deem dishonourable in all those years. It seems very old-fashioned now, that attitude. In a way, when you came back, it gave her back to him. You're very like her, you know. So when you offended against all his so dearly held principles, it was like losing Diana all over again, and worse. Can you understand that?"

"Yes, only too well. I wish I'd known all this before."

"When he discovered that he'd done you an injustice, he was terribly upset. For all his faults, he's a fair-minded man, and to think he'd treated Diana's daughter unjustly and harshly, the daughter he'd promised her to look after, was a betrayal of all his past. As I said, at heart he's a very simple man."

"Yes. Why didn't Angus tell me all this when he came down to ask me to go back?"

"He didn't know. Most of this happened before Angus was born, remember, and it was just taken for granted that Aunt Diana was a friend of the family. I was the only one who knew, and perhaps my mother guessed, but one respects people's right to the privacy of their hearts."

"If I'd known, I wouldn't have written him that letter."

"In the circumstances, and knowing no more than you did, I think it was a pretty generous effort," said Harriet drily.

"You see, I didn't want to lose my independence again. And I don't want to now."

"I can appreciate that. Don't I wish I'd fought for mine when I was young! But it needn't be threatened this time. If you'll just come and stay until you've restored the old man's peace of mind, and then keep in touch with him, it needn't threaten your independence of action again. You're writing, so I hear. Tell me about it."

Linda did so, feeling herself for the first time close to this woman who had hitherto seemed so reserved and unapproachable.

"It's only a modest beginning, but I have hopes," concluded Linda.

"Your father was gifted. You may be able to use a similar talent to better effect. I'll see that you have a room of your own to work in while you're with us. Then, later, if you want to leave Hartfield, perhaps you could find a place not too far off so that you could see Father regularly. It would mean so much to him. I never thought I'd live to hear myself pleading so eloquently for him. He's left a trail of broken crowns behind him in his time."

"How old were you when your mother died and you took over the reins, Miss Ferndale?"

"Nineteen. I wanted to take an arts degree and teach. My father has always thought a woman's place was in the home, and I wasn't strong enough to fight him. Too young, perhaps. We were at war then and I had to be contented with the local ARP work and trying to run Hartfield without help and look after Father, who was frantically busy. Oh well, it's all a long

243

time ago. In a way, you and I were in similar situations. If your father had lived to be old, you would have grown middle-aged, too, looking after him. And in far harder circumstances than I ever knew."

"My father was a kind man."

"Which would have made your chains even stronger. Stuart had an appealing manner. He invited mothering."

"Yes. I could never have left him to look after himself. It would have finished him. He had so little."

"And now, perhaps, you see your freedom threatened again? Soft hearts are always vulnerable. But you shan't be trapped a second time. That I promise you."

"Thank you," said Linda, and, as she met Harriet's dark eyes, knew that she had found an ally and an understanding friend where she would have least expected it.

"Well, I won't keep you any longer. You'll have things to pack. Arrangements to make." She stooped to smell the bowl of primroses on the window sill. "You've a cosy little retreat here. Angus led me to expect a bleak cell. I'd have given a lot for it at your age. A place of your own to work in without distraction."

"How are you getting back to Bude?"

"Angus is picking me up at the church at twelve-thirty. I'll have a walk round until then."

"Can I come with you? I'd like some air, and there are better things to study than accounts on a sunny March morning."

They walked along the cliffs, talking about books and writing. It was a blustery day and the sea was flecked with white horses. Below them, the surf sparkled and danced in the sun as it washed over the sand, and gulls planed along in the wind, soaring and dipping, their cries the counterpoint to the breaking of the waves. The grass beneath their feet shone in the sun and everything that day looked washed and clean, and as they walked and talked, Linda was conscious of a sense of beginning again, of starting a new chapter. Was conscious, too, of the comfort of this un-expected companionship which felt like a firm hand in hers. Nothing cosy about Harriet Ferndale, but an honest directness and an intelligent understanding which were as reassuring as the spring sunshine.

Here, she felt, was a counsellor she could rely on, and would need, for in going back to Hartfield she was venturing again on dangerous ground, with the problems of her relationship with Angus now wide open again instead of safely despatched, to say nothing of the bridge she now had to cross to meet his grandfather again.

"How odd life is!" she said, as they turned back. "I've spent all these past months painfully carving out a future for myself and had just completed the picture, and now in a few hours it's completely changed. I'd put Hartfield and all the Ferndales out of my life for ever, I thought, and now I'm thrown right back amongst them. And I've found a friend in the enemy camp, too," she added with an odd little smile that seemed to touch her companion, for Harriet said:

"An unexpected bonus for me, too, my dear, at a time of life when such bonuses are rare. I'm very glad I came, though Angus assured me that I was wasting my time."

"Perhaps because where he had failed, he couldn't imagine anyone else succeeding," said Linda in such a dry tone that Harriet shot a quick look at her and then smiled.

"Men are indeed the vainer sex. I gather that you and my nephew are not on good terms."

"We're certainly not."

"He can be unusually exasperating. Strong-willed, like his grandfather, but with a good many saving graces. I'm fond of him."

But Angus was too sore a subject for Linda to discuss, and she began to talk about her parents, seeking more enlightenment about the past, for the story had stirred her deeply. Her mother had always been so gay. Whatever unhappiness she had felt in her heart, her husband and daughter had never been made to suffer. She remembered that her mother had always treated her father like a child. Impossible to conceive that she and Luke Ferndale had been so deeply committed to each other.

But as they neared the church, Linda felt uneasy at meeting Angus again. No word had passed between them since the return of the book, but now, on this morning which had revealed more than anything the limitations of understanding between people, she felt on unsure ground. She remembered the last words he had said to her. "If and when you're ready to come out of your bolt-hole, we'll fight it out." Now circumstances were forcing her out of her retreat, and she felt unprepared and confused.

The car was waiting by the church, and as they approached, Angus got out. He stood by the car door, waiting for them, his expression austere, to say the least. Linda was annoyed to feel her heart beating more quickly as she met his steady gaze.

"Linda's agreed to come back with us tomorrow, Angus," said Harriet.

"Really? Congratulations on your powers of persuasion, Aunt Harriet," he said drily. "Will you be ready at nine o'clock tomorrow morning, Linda?"

"Yes."

"Right."

He walked round the car and opened the door for his aunt, and exchanged no more words with Linda. As she watched the car drive off down the lane, her resolution stiffened. Stung by the cold disapproval of his attitude, she was more than ever determined not to weaken in the face of the undoubted attraction which he held for her, and for many others, she guessed. He had the looks, the voice, the careless arrogance, which made up a strong challenge to any girl, and he traded on it. A present should have had her running back to him in gratitude, the silly girl so liable to lose her head with men. She should have been grateful for his patronage again. But she could not find for him the excuses she could find for his grandfather, for Angus's picture of her had been the more contemptible. An unforeseen tide had swept her back into the Ferndale circle again, but to Angus she would not yield an inch.

19

Caterpillar in the rose

AND thus it was a year almost to a day after her first return to Hartfield that Linda found herself driving through the stone pillars of its entrance once again, and remembered that last occasion as though it had happened to a different person, so much had happened in the year between.

During the long journey from Cornwall, Angus had said as little to her as politeness demanded, his attitude maddeningly formal. She had sat in the back with Harriet, glad of her company, still a little bewildered at this sudden turn of events. They had stopped for lunch at a country hotel not far from Salisbury, but Linda had found herself with little appetite for food, excellent though it was. There was something about the mocking gleam in Angus's black eyes and his imperturbable, chilly courtesy that upset her digestion. She was glad when tea-time found them at their journey's end.

If during that journey she had wondered just how her meeting with old Mr. Ferndale would go off and what she should say to him, when the time came there was no difficulty at all. He must have been watching for them at the window, for as soon as they were inside the front door, he appeared from the drawing-room, wheeling himself in an invalid chair. Linda, shocked at his haggard, gaunt appearance, and moved by his expression, took the two hands he held out to her and stooped quickly to kiss his cheek, saying softly:

"I'm so sorry, Uncle Luke. I'd have come before if I'd known."

"My dear," he said gruffly, "it's wonderful to see you. Thank you for coming. When Harriet telephoned yesterday to tell me, I was overjoyed. I've lots to say to you, but not now. You must all be wanting some tea. Good journey, Angus?"

"Yes, thanks, Grandfather. How are you feeling?"

"Better. A lot better. Now don't start fussing, Harriet. I can wheel myself back to the fire." Then, as an afterthought, he patted his daughter's hand and said abruptly, "Thank you, my dear."

Angus got up to go immediately after tea.

"Must you drive back to town this evening, dear?" asked Harriet. "Why not stay the night and go up in the morning? You've done enough driving for one day."

"Sorry. I have to be in the office first thing tomorrow morning. Goodbye, Grandfather. Take things quietly."

"How else can I take 'em? Stuck in this confounded chair."

"I was thinking of mental excitement, not physical. I'll be down next week-end."

"Thank you, my boy. Mind how you go. Bad to drive when you're tired. So many lunatics on the road nowadays."

"Too true. Goodbye, Linda."

He gave her a cool nod and went out, his aunt following him. A few minutes later, Linda heard the sound of the car driving off, but Harriet Ferndale did not return.

Luke leaned forward in his chair, his hands on his knees, and said:

"Linda, my dear, what can I say about that appalling episode in Bermuda? I did you a grave injustice, and am more deeply

252

sorry than I can tell you. My daughter-in-law, it seems, went out of her way to paint a black picture of you, and that foolish young man . . . Well, it's no use going over the sorry business any more. I was misled, but I should have had more confidence in you, should have listened to you. I ought to have known that Diana's daughter was not a liar. That letter you wrote me—the first one when you ran away —was like your mother reproaching me. It's what she would have said."

"Let's forget it. The case looked black against me. I don't blame you. When I wrote refusing to come back, it wasn't only because of what happened in Bermuda, it was because I didn't want to lose my freedom and independence again. You had rather . . . annexed me. I couldn't put myself in that position again, and I still can't. In fairness to you, I must make that clear."

"I know. I know. Harriet drove that home yesterday when she telephoned me. Don't know why you young people are so touchy about your independence. Angus is the same."

"And weren't you the same when you were young?"

"Of course. But I had duties to my elders which I respected. That's old-fashioned now. A thing of the past."

"Is it?" asked Linda gently. "I don't think your daughter has ever forgotten her duty to you, and I don't think I forgot mine to my father."

He looked at her sharply, his grey eyes as shrewd and penetrating as ever they were. Then he gave her a wry smile.

"Diana had exactly that gentle way of reproving me, with those soft dark eyes of hers watching me like yours. Always infuriated me and made me feel guilty. You've found your tongue since you were last here, young woman. And just what does your declaration of independence mean?"

"That I can't come back here permanently to live. But I won't go far away again, and I'll always come when you want me."

"I see. Will you spend the summer here? I could play on your pity and say I don't expect to see the summer out, but I won't. Not fair. But give me this summer, Linda. An Indian summer for me. You shall be

254

free to do just as you wish here. I'll make no demands. But just to have you about the place . . . would mean so much to me."

It seemed especially cruel, she thought, to see a man of his powerful physique confined to a wheel-chair. The massive, stooped shoulders, the rugged head, the strong, knotted hands were never made for a cage. Suffering had etched even deeper furrows on his craggy face, but the eyes were challenging still. He might be stricken, but he was not of the stuff to be defeated.

"Yes," she said with a smile. "We'll share the summer. I'd like that."

"Thank you, my dear. After I threw you away—it's generous of you. But Diana was always generous. Never bore a grudge. Could flare up a bit, but it was all over and done with quickly—never let it rankle. It was a terrible loss for both of us when she died—that should have been a bond between us. But your father took you away. I mustn't hark on it and bore you, though. Old men live in the past. But somehow, you are my past. You're so like her. Doing some writing, Harriet tells me. I admire your spunk in getting up after that knock-out and setting about making a new life for yourself. Tell me about this writing."

She told him about her life in the chalet and the book she had written. When Harriet rejoined them later, they were deep in a discussion of Trollope, Luke Ferndale's favourite author.

As the weeks slipped by, Linda found herself surprised by the easy way in which she became part of the life at Hartfield, in contrast with that first attempt a year ago. Then she had felt awkward, patronised, uncertain. Now she felt at home, warmed by Harriet's support and friendship, and the very real affection which was growing between her and Luke. It seemed to her that illness had softened him, but Harriet observed drily one day, in reply to Linda's observation to that effect:

"Not illness, my dear. You. This love affair between my father and you Dawley females has no ending. It's incredible. A sort of Heathcliff obsession. You wouldn't believe it outside of Emily Brontë. He's changed enormously since you've been here. It makes me wonder how different he would have been if he'd married your mother in the first place. Happiness does more for the character than frustration, even with a puritan like my father."

"I enjoy his company. He's stubborn and argumentative sometimes, but he has such a shrewd, lively mind. He talks a lot of the past, and has a knack of bringing it alive. Sometimes he forgets and calls me Diana, and I feel strange, as though I've gone back in time."

"Well, don't get too immersed in his dream world. Perhaps it's as well to have Angus here at week-ends to bring you back to reality. Why are you two at daggers drawn? I can almost feel the electricity in the air when you're in the same room."

"His attitude infuriates me."

"When Angus uses that silky politeness of his as a weapon, it's far more devastating than any blunt instrument, I agree. But why? I thought you and he hit it off pretty well when you were here last year."

"That was in my salad days," said Linda lightly.

"Well, it's none of my business, but he'd beat you in a fight, my dear. Much better stay out of the arena altogether if you can't be friends."

"That's what I meant to do, but he won't let me. He trails his coat for me. If he wants to fight, I'm not going to let him score without retaliating. He's too sure of himself."

Harriet looked at Linda's flushed face and said laconically:

"Angus has one great advantage, dear. He knows exactly what he's doing, and why he's doing it. Do you?"

Linda threw up her hands and smiled ruefully.

"I'm going to do some work on my book. My characters are much easier to handle than Angus Ferndale."

But for once she could not lose herself in her writing, and Harriet's reminder of her tormentor stayed with her until in desperation she put her work aside and went out into the garden to seek Amos, whose presence was always both astringent and comforting. In a bewildering world, he seemed to stand for the basic certainties of life. Nothing, she felt, would ever surprise or shock Amos, or throw him off his balance. Perhaps he could impart a little of his imperviousness to her on this sunny

June morning when his domain was looking at its best.

She lingered by the wide border watching a bumble-bee nuzzling into a large, pink, blowsy peony. Some near-by pinks scented the air, and a blackbird foraged among them to add more grubs to the collection already in his beak. How he could add even one more without dropping the lot she did not know, but he added several before flying off to the nest built in the japonica just below her bedroom window. Why could she not dismiss Angus instead of feeling him like a prickly burr in the smooth pattern of her days? Life had never been so pleasantly arranged: she worked undistracted in her own study every morning, she spent every afternoon with Uncle Luke, she had Harriet's friendship to enjoy, and a degree of comfort and beauty in her surroundings which made her fortunate indeed. All was harmony, except for Angus. It was an absurd state of affairs. She could neither break his mocking urbanity nor ignore it. It stung her like a wasp and she knew that he knew it stung her. He came down every week-end to see his grandfather, and every Friday she found her nerves pricking in anticipation. Tomorrow, she thought, she would have it out with him.

Amos was stooping over one of the rose bushes, frowning, although the roses were blooming freely and to Linda looked worthy of a prize at any show. Experience told her, however, that Amos saw things through more critical eyes. Sun or snow, he was never without the felt hat, and he wore it tilted forward that morning as though to narrow his gaze on the offending object.

"Good morning, Amos. Aren't they a lovely sight?"

"Them dratted caterpillars are doing their spoiling work. Look at this—half-way into the bud." He removed the green caterpillar and trod on it. "I sprayed 'em, too. Once they get to this stage, though, you can't get at 'em except with your fingers. Cunning, the way they roll themselves up and stick the leaves together round them."

"What a pleasant life, to live and feed on roses. I wonder if roses taste as nice as they look."

Amos's vivid blue eyes surveyed her in

silence for a moment. Such frivolous obser-
vations, she felt, were not approved of.

"Did you borrow my small secateurs
yesterday, Lindey?"

"Er, yes. I cut some roses for Mr.
Ferndale's room."

"And left 'em in the garden-room in the
trug, wet, under a pile of dead leaves. Took
me quarter of an hour this morning to find
them."

"Oh, I'm sorry, Amos. I took the roses
in and forgot I hadn't put the secateurs
back."

"When people borrow my tools, I expect
them to be put back in their proper place,
wiped and greased if they've got wet. And
the beech leaves in the trug should have
been put on the compost heap."

"Yes, Amos. I'm sorry, really. I got
talking to Mr. Ferndale, and forgot."

"Don't like slovenly habits. Good tools
deserve good treatment, and a garden's not
just a place to cut flowers from, you know."

"Oh, I do know. It's a kingdom, Amos.
Your kingdom. And I broke the rules. Let
me do some work to make amends. Shall
I dead-head the roses in the floribunda

beds? I noticed the rain had spoiled a few blooms."

She smiled at him, her head on one side, and his brown wizened face relaxed into the nearest Amos ever came to smiling.

"Aye, Lindey Lou, you've a soft way with you. Always had. If you want a job, you can go over these bushes one by one and where there's a leaf folded up, there's your caterpillar. Squash it."

"Not nearly as pleasant as cutting off dead roses."

"Can't pick and choose. This job's more urgent. Then I can get on with mending the fruit cage or them devils of birds'll have all the strawberries."

"Poor Amos. Always having to wage war on the enemy. You never seem to have time to enjoy the results. Just look at this rose. Isn't it perfection? The loveliest shape, half open. Petals like red velvet and smelling like Paradise."

"Aye, that's a good old rose. Crimson Glory. Scorches a bit in the sun, though."

"Oh, Amos," protested Linda, laughing. "Never perfection. Always a reservation. You've produced a bed of magnificent roses. Gloat over them."

"Modern roses don't have the form of the old 'uns. Strong, I grant you, but flowers as big as cabbages and poor scent, most of 'em. Now Madame Butterfly, that's a rose," he said, fingering a blush pink bloom in the next bed. "Shape, colour, scent—a real elegant rose. Nothing vulgar about it. I remember it in my first garden when I was a boy learning the job, so it's been going for forty or fifty years. They don't come like that now. Tastes are different. Bigger and brighter, that's what they want now. But this has the real classic style. Pity the thrips like it so much."

"I knew there must be one snag. Do I have to squash the caterpillars? If I throw them on the grass, the birds can have them. I'm sure they'll be glad of them with so many young to feed now."

"The only good caterpillar is a dead caterpillar. And I'm not so fond of birds, neither. *And* I've no more time to waste chatting, Lindey. You always was one to get me chatting but I've got work to do. When you've done the caterpillars, you can dead-head the roses, and remember what I said about the secateurs."

"Yes, Amos," said Linda meekly as she started her tour of inspection.

It seemed wrong to be killing anything on a morning like this, even caterpillars, but she knew better than to express such illogical foolishness to Amos. If she wanted roses, she must kill caterpillars. That was all there was to it. She was a muddle-headed sentimentalist and ought to try to be more clear-minded, which brought her back to Angus. Ruthless and clear-minded. Bother Angus. He would keep intruding. Hardening her heart, she pinched a folded rose leaf between her fingers without investigating further, wishing that she could obliterate Angus from her thoughts in like manner.

20

Summer week-end

"GOOD morning, Linda," said Angus as he joined her for breakfast.

"Oh, good morning." She turned startled eyes to him. "I didn't know you were here."

"No? I arrived in the early hours of this morning."

So that explained the telephone call she had heard just after she had gone to bed the previous evening.

"I thought Aunt Harriet said you wouldn't be here until lunch-time."

"That was the original plan. I changed it."

She knew he wouldn't explain, and she wouldn't ask him. He picked up the paper and was glancing at it when his aunt came in.

"Oh, you're down, Angus. I thought you

might be late in view of the hour at which you arrived. Did you enjoy the concert?"

"Very much, thanks. Hope I didn't wake you when I arrived. It seemed the most sensible arrangement in the circumstances."

"Yes. I didn't hear you come in. You must have crept upstairs; I'm a light sleeper and I had half an ear open for you."

"Ah, I learnt that trick years ago. How's Grandfather?"

"Amazingly well. We've got a male nurse for him. He didn't like Nurse Stockwell, you know."

"Don't blame him. Too cheerful by half."

"Well, Stevens, that's the male nurse, looks as morose as a bloodhound, but he seems a kind, efficient man and Father seems to have taken to him quite well. And now, my dear, what would you like for breakfast?"

"Bacon and tomatoes. I fixed it with Ethel just now. You fruit juice and toast and marmalade people are too frugal for me."

"What did you hear at the concert?"

"Schubert. Very lyrical. And Shostakovich. Very stirring. Gave my companion an excellent appetite for supper afterwards, which was why I was even later than I expected to be. Marmalade, Linda?"

"Thank you."

"I've promised to turn out for the Edenmere cricket team this afternoon, Aunt Harriet," said Angus. "Think the old man would like to come, as it looks like being a decent day?"

"Yes, I'm sure he would. When did you fix this, Angus? I didn't know you played cricket these days."

"I don't. Haven't played for some years, but I had an appeal from your worthy headmaster when I met him in the village last week-end. He said they were finding it difficult to raise an eleven this season and asked me if I'd play for the home matches while I was spending week-ends at Hartfield. He seems to take his duties as president very seriously. He thought it might give Grandfather an added interest, too. Didn't he tell you? I thought you might have discussed it with him."

"No. I haven't seen Philip this week. I think it's a good idea. We'll all come and watch. What do you say, Linda?"

"Let's not impose it on Linda. She'd probably be glad of an afternoon off from the Ferndales. It's a boring game to watch unless, like Grandfather, you've played yourself."

"It will be a new experience for me," said Linda smoothly.

"On your heads be it."

Angus went off to see his grandfather immediately after breakfast. The old man breakfasted in bed, the only concession he made to invalidism, and did not appear until mid-morning. When Angus had gone, Linda said:

"Why did Angus choose to come in the early hours?"

"Oh, he was taking some girl to a concert, and as she lives near Ellarton, half-way here, it seemed sensible for him to come on to Hartfield after seeing her home."

"One way and another, he leads a busy life," said Linda drily.

"Well, I've a couple of Philip's boys coming for some coaching this morning," said Harriet. "I must be off. How's the book coming on?"

"A bit sticky. Doesn't seem to flow like the first."

"Perhaps you've other things on your mind. You're doing wonderful work with Father, anyway, my dear. I appreciate that."

"We enjoy being together. You're a very generous-minded person, Aunt Harriet. You've given up your life to looking after Uncle Luke and Hartfield, and I don't think you've had much appreciation for it. Then I come along and spend a few hours a day with him, enjoying myself into the bargain, and he makes so much fuss of me that I'm ashamed. A lot of women in your position would resent that, but you thank me, and are so good to me. You're the one who's earned the laurels, not I."

"It was my duty. And Father's not the only one to like having you around, dear. You've brought a new warmth to this house. Now for these boys. I'll hammer some knowledge of their native language into their heads if it's the last thing I do," said Harriet briskly.

Linda did not see Angus again until shortly before lunch, when she met him in the garden pushing his grandfather's invalid chair along the path between the borders.

"Good morning, Uncle Luke," she said, smiling and kissing him. "Did you have a good night?"

" Middling. Kept trying to work out how it was you managed to beat me at chess yesterday evening when you're only a beginner and I've been playing all my life."

"I think you let me win, just to encourage me."

"No. I underestimated my opponent and wasn't giving the game the concentration it needs. This is the man I can't ever relax with, though. Angus. A real battle of wits."

"I can imagine it. I don't think chess would ever be my game."

"You act too hastily, Linda, no doubt," said Angus. "Then when you're in a corner, get reckless."

"As a matter of fact, that's just what she does do," said Luke Ferndale, chuckling. "I've been telling Angus that we ought to try and make things a little livelier for you here, dear. You mustn't let an old man monopolise you. There's a tennis court here. Why don't you two play? Get Harriet to invite some young people."

"I'm very happy just as things are, Uncle Luke. I love the country and walking and the garden. I'm finding this a halcyon summer, and I don't want any entertaining. My time is fully occupied and most happily."

"That's as may be, but you're young and you need a little fun. Harriet's bought tickets for a charity dance in Rolgate, next Saturday. She doesn't intend to use them. Just felt she had to support the cause. Take Linda, Angus."

Angus's black eyes met Linda's above the old man's head. There was a wicked gleam in them but his face gave nothing away as he said:

"Does that really appeal to you, Linda?"

"Appeal to her? Of course it does. Why shouldn't it?" demanded Luke.

"Why not indeed?" murmured Angus.

Luke was beginning to look at them suspiciously, a frown creasing his forehead, and Linda quickly threw the ball back to Angus.

"You won't be free that evening, will you, Angus? Didn't you say something about seeing a friend in Ellarton?"

271

"No," said Angus blandly. "If you would like to go, I'm at your service."

"That's settled, then," said Luke. "And arrange some tennis, Angus. You're only young once. Enjoy yourselves while you're fit."

"What about those puritan principles of yours, Grandfather? Don't tell me you're slipping."

"I've always believed in sport and exercise for mental and physical well-being, my boy, as you know. I'm not against enjoyment, if it's the right kind. I shall enjoy seeing you play cricket again. Pity you let it go. You were a stylish bat. I wonder you keep as fit as you do, in London. Get any exercise in the week?"

"I belong to a squash club, and work off my sins on an occasional game."

"Glad to hear it." Luke pulled out his hunter watch. "Nearly lunch-time. We'd better get back to the house. You look pretty in that yellow dress, Linda. Colour of primroses. It was a favourite colour with your mother, I remember."

The Edenmere cricket ground was bounded on one side by a row of old lime trees, and here, in the pattern of sunshine and shadow beneath them, sat a scattering of spectators, among them the Ferndales. Away on their right, beyond the low wooden posts and rails that marked the boundary of that side of the ground, stretched a meadow in which cows were grazing, their heavy flanks burnished by the sun. On the third side, a large wooden pavilion backed by beech trees housed some white-flannelled figures who spilled over to the wooden seats in front. Two small boys kept score on a blackboard near by. A low hedge of hawthorn made the fourth boundary, which divided the cricket ground from the grounds of Philip Hanwood's preparatory school. The village lay beyond the meadow, its church spire just visible above a coppice on the far side. It was, Linda thought, as pretty a cricket ground as could be found anywhere in the English countryside.

The scent from the lime blossoms was sweet on the air, and she leaned back in her deck-chair so that her face was in the shade and let a delicious feeling of idle content wash over her. In all the changing pace and pattern of modern life, village cricket teams carried on much as they always had, and it pleased her, although the game itself meant little to her. The smack of the ball, the spattering of hand-claps for a boundary, the occasional lively and more vociferous response from a group of villagers perched like birds along the post-and-rails boundary, the white figures of the players against the sun-bright grass, a day when the English summer displayed itself at its best. The brittle sophistication of her life in the hotel in Bermuda now seemed strangely unreal. The simple country life for me, she thought. This is my world. The English countryside and its traditions, its values rooted in basic truths; lives lived close to natural creation, attuned to the seasons. The enduring things, that comforted and sustained the spirit. Slowly, she felt she was finding her way; discovering what really mattered to her; discovering, too, the folly of hasty judgment and the penalties of pride.

She watched Angus run for a ball, pick it up, turn and throw a wicket down with a speed which drew loud applause from the post-and-rails section. He had always moved well, with that swift co-ordination which made everything look so easy. Not a rabid games player, he had natural physical advantages which would enable him to give a creditable display at any sport; something to do with a rapport between eye and limb. His mother had displayed the same quality on the tennis court. If Angus had wished, he could no doubt have excelled at any sport he chose to concentrate on, but he seemed to prefer a dilettante attitude to sport, enjoying whatever came his way if he was in the mood.

She wished that she could bring a cool objective judgment to her feeling about Angus. She had determined to dismiss him, but he had never been far from her mind. A growing feeling of guilt at the way she had returned his present warred with the recollection of that afternoon in the Caythorpe Hotel when he had reduced her feeling for him to a cheap little infatuation, the prelude to flitting off to an affair with another man. If they could have a row and be done with it, the atmosphere would be easier than this barbed holding-off, but he never varied his cool, almost mocking politeness, and in all these weeks he had never really talked to her at all. She might

275

have been a stranger except for the challenging gleam in his eye and the purpose she sensed behind it. She felt that he was driving her into a corner. Well, she could be stubborn, too. But in the happy calm that now prevailed at Hartfield, it was a pity to have one buzzing wasp, she thought, as she watched him chase a ball.

During the afternoon, several people came up to exchange a few words with Luke, and when they wheeled him round to the pavilion side for tea, he was accorded VIP treatment, for it was Luke Ferndale who had given the club its new pavilion after the old one had been blown down one night in a gale. Angus joined them, but managed to avoid saying anything to Linda although he brought her a second cup of tea and handed it to her with a polite smile. All through her conversation with Philip Hanwood about the craft of writing, she was conscious of Angus's deep, slightly husky voice beside her discussing the finer points of cricket with his grandfather.

Angus, who had asked to go in late in the batting order, narrowly survived being run out for a duck by his companion, but then went on to score a lively twenty-two not out, giving the home side a narrow victory.

"Not bad. Not bad at all," was his grandfather's verdict.

After supper that evening, after Luke had gone to bed and Harriet had left them, Linda tried to screw up her courage to have it out with Angus, thinking that the day's sport might have put him in a more genial mood towards her, but before she could frame the first words in the battle, he said smoothly:

"I'm sorry the old man has forced you into this dance next week. I'll make it as painless as I can for you. He has to be humoured."

He made for the door and she said desperately:

"Angus."

He paused, his eyebrows raised, surveying her with an ironical expression.

"It doesn't matter," she said curtly, and he went.

She ran her hands through her hair despairingly, feeling the need for some violent outlet for her feelings.

"Hullo," said Harriet, coming in a few

minutes later. "You look as though you've been blown through a hedge."

"Not blown through. Just bounced off, and it was a thorn hedge."

On Sunday afternoon, sitting on the lawn in the shade of the copper beech tree, Linda was reading the last chapter of *Barchester Towers* to Luke. The mastiff lay beside them, his grey muzzle resting on Linda's foot. Until Angus had arrived a few minutes earlier, she had been enjoying the book, but although she turned her head away from the long figure lying prone on the grass near by, she was acutely conscious of his presence, which broke her absorption.

"Excellent," said Luke Ferndale when she closed the book. "Nobody like Trollope for a fine, rounded story. And you're a good reader, my dear. A nice voice for it."

"I used to read a lot to my father when his sight failed. Jason, you're giving me pins and needles," she added as she lifted the heavy head of the dog from her foot, caressed it, and laid it gently down in the grass. Jason was old and had to be treated with consideration.

"What a lovely week-end this is!" said Luke. "The sort of summer days one dreams of in November. Must say Amos keeps the garden very well. Those delphiniums— lovely colour. Must be a terrible thing, to lose your sight. Providence is being very kind to give me a summer like this."

"We have had some wet days," said Linda, smiling.

"I haven't noticed them."

"Do you want the *Sunday Times*, Grandfather?" asked Angus, pulling it from behind his head.

"No, thanks. Don't seem to want to read newspapers these days. Full of depressing, shocking things."

"Trollope's world is less complex," observed Angus, subsiding again.

"That poem you were reading to me the other day, Linda," said Luke. "The one about the late lark singing. I've been trying to remember it. How does it go? Can you remember?"

"Only the last verse,

So be my passing!
My task accomplish'd, and the long day done,

279

My wages taken, and in my heart
Some late lark singing,
Let me be gathered to the quiet west,
The sundown splendid and serene,
Death.

But I'll get the book for you."

"No, dear, don't worry now. That was the verse that's been haunting me. Some late lark singing. Never been a reader of poetry, but that somehow hit a deep chord. Who wrote it?"

"W. E. Henley. The 'I am the master of my fate' man. I think he's your sort of poet, Uncle Luke."

"Yes. I should have read more poetry, perhaps. Always thought it high falutin' stuff. I know you love it. But then your father educated you there, no doubt. A late lark singing. That's what you are to me, my dear. A song I never expected."

Moved, Linda had no words, but she laid her hand on his for a moment. A faint wind stirred the branches of the beech and brought movement to the pattern of dappled sunshine and shadow around them. Jason snapped lethargically at a buzzing fly, and Luke tilted his panama hat forward against a shaft of sunlight. Linda leaned back in her deck-chair and watched a yellow butterfly fluttering on the border of lavender beneath the terrace. A trance-like serenity seemed to wrap them in silence. It wasn't until the church clock struck four and a rattle of tea-cups could be heard that Linda sat up and caught Angus's gaze. His expression broke the spell as effectively as a bucket of cold water thrown over her. A late lark singing, indeed, after all she had said to him of the Ferndales. She could read it in letters a foot high from the wry twist of his mouth and the look in his eyes. She jumped up and ran across the lawn to help Harriet wheel the tea trolley. He spelt it out again just before he left that night.

"I notice it's Uncle Luke and Aunt Harriet now. You're quite one of the family, Linda. A trifle inconsistent, aren't you?"

"I always used to call your grandfather uncle when I was a child, and your aunt asked me to drop the Miss Ferndale."

"That wasn't really what I meant, was it?"

"I don't know what you mean, Angus."

"I think you do."

"Tell me," she said angrily.

"No. You're going to tell me, in your own time. Goodbye. Enjoy your halo."

Which was, she thought as he went out to his car, just about the nastiest shot of all.

21

Landfall

ROLGATE was a small town six or seven miles from Edenmere, and the dance was held in the community hall. It was an informal affair organised by Edenmere and neighbouring villages to raise funds for their cottage hospital.

The last time she had danced with Angus had been at the Viennese dance at the hotel, a very grand affair compared with this, but she hoped that the recollection of that evening would soften his attitude to her, make him more approachable. The simple lime-green silk dress which she had bought in Ellarton that week gave her confidence. It was the first dress she had bought since her return, almost wardrobe-less, from Bermuda. Dancing together, he must unbend, she thought as she fastened the pearl necklace which had been her mother's.

Angus, waiting for her downstairs, greeted her with the same formality which he had maintained ever since her return, but she was not unduly dejected. On the dance floor, in his arms, it would be different.

It had not occurred to her for one moment that he would not dance with her that evening, and when he introduced her to a party which included some of the Edenmere cricket team, she did not suspect that he was opting out. But somehow, she found herself dancing her first dance with a fair-haired young man with a red face and the physique of a weight-lifter, whom she remembered as the top scorer in the cricket match, and thereafter he monopolised her, Angus having apparently vanished into thin air.

Her partner's name was George Lyall, and it was not long before she discovered that he had two passions in life, cars and cricket, to the exclusion, it seemed, of all else. As neither of these topics roused in Linda more than an interest so faint as to be invisible, the conversation was very one-sided, a fact which seemed in no way to dim her partner's enthusiasm. Coupled with the fact that he was an atrocious dancer, Linda's anger with Angus grew stronger as the evening progressed and George remained devoted to her.

"I can't think where Angus is," she said, as George brought her a sandwich and a cup of coffee in the interval.

"Didn't you know? He's gone to the concert at the town hall, just round the corner."

"*What?*"

"Yes. Surely he told you. Some chamber music group, playing Beethoven quartets, I believe he said. Sounded ghastly to me. You didn't think he was staying for the dance, did you?"

He stared at her curiously, and she said hastily:

"I didn't really know. Angus was a bit vague about it, but of course, I remember now, he doesn't like dances." She turned a dazzling smile on George to hide her wrath and confusion, and added, "Do you?"

"Well, I'm not much of a dancing man, but I enjoy a hop with a pretty partner like you," he said gallantly. "I was odd man out and was glad when Angus said you'd be solo and he'd be glad if I'd keep an eye on you. For that, I'll stand him a drink after the next match. He played a useful game last Saturday, didn't he? Pleased old Mr. Ferndale, I bet."

And with the conversation safely back to cricket, all Linda had to do was sip her coffee and listen while she simmered inside at Angus's treachery.

By the end of the evening, with one ankle bruised and bones in several other quarters aching, for George put much energy into his dancing, Linda knew all about the relative merits of at least six makes of cars and the performances of so many West Indian and Australian cricketers that she wondered if she was mistaken in thinking that George was an office worker and not either a professional cricketer or a sports reporter. With a whole new vocabulary in her mind and black anger in her heart, she could scarcely contain herself when Angus appeared half-way through the last waltz. She saw him over George's shoulder, and her hand tightened on her partner, who took this as a sign of encouragement and drew her closer in his bear-like hug.

Angus lit a cigarette and surveyed the throng as though he found the sight faintly incredible. Insufferable, superior, auto-cratic brute, she thought passionately. He smiled and raised a hand in salute as George swept her past him, but Linda closed her eyes, praying for self-control, and stumbled as George's erratic idea of time veered farther from the beat than usual.

"Sorry," he said cheerfully. "We've not done badly together, have we? You're light on your feet and easy to dance with. Some girls feel like sacks of cement. What about me driving you home? No need to bother Angus. I could show you the MG's paces."

"Another time, George, thank you. I'd better go back with Angus now that he's waited."

"Wish I'd thought of it sooner. We needn't have bothered him to wait for you after the concert. Sure you won't change your mind?"

"Quite sure. I've something I want to discuss with Angus. Thank you, all the same."

"What about a spin tomorrow, then?"

"I'm sorry, George. Sundays I like to spend with old Mr. Ferndale. You know how it is."

"Sure. Pitiful seeing the old boy like

that. He's always been such a power in the land. Used to be scared stiff of him when I was a boy. Old Ferney. A regular Tartar. Done a lot for the village, though. One of the old school. Sorry."

This time it was the other ankle and she tried not to limp as they walked off the floor for the last time.

"Thanks for providing me with such a nice partner, Angus" said George, a broad smile on his face. "You're nuts, preferring Beethoven, my lad."

"Well, I can see you've enjoyed yourselves," observed Angus.

"And did you enjoy the concert?" asked Linda coolly, but her voice trembled a little.

"Very much."

In the car park, George put an arm round her and gave her a hug before roaring off in his MG.

"You seem to have made a hit there," said Angus, opening the door of his car for her.

Ignoring this pleasantry, she got in and kicked off her shoes, feeling as though her toes would never be the same again. In the interests of road safety, she bottled up her feelings until they arrived back, maintaining a stony silence during the journey. When he brought the car to a stop outside the house, however, she turned on him like a spitting cat.

"How dared you do that to me, Angus!"

"Do what?"

"Leave me high and dry at that dance."

"I left you with potential partners. Surely, in the circumstances, that was the best I could do in order to relieve you of my objectionable company. The dance was more or less forced on us by Grandfather, but I know how much you dislike having to associate with me. You made it so clear, remember? In our interview in your shack that day, and, in case I hadn't got the message loud and clear, by returning my present without comment. That being so, I should have thought you'd be grateful at the way I removed myself tonight."

"Without telling me beforehand?"

"Did that matter? The important thing was to be rid of me. I'm sorry if George didn't prove a pleasant companion. He's a decent chap. Anyway, there were others. You can't blame me if you weren't well suited."

"Oh, you're detestable!"

"I really can't see why you're so angry. Is it, by any chance, that you find yourself hoist with your own petard?"

"I should have thought," she said, ignoring this awkward question, "that while I'm living at Hartfield, you might at least make an effort to be agreeable."

"But I've been making great efforts. Politeness has been my watch-word, and what I did tonight was in line with your own wishes that were expressed with great clarity and subsequently underlined when I extended an olive branch. What *are* you complaining about, Linda?"

"Oh, I hate you in this ironical mood. That was months ago."

"You've taken nothing back."

"You've kept me at a distance all the time. You've not once really talked to me since I came back here."

"Why should I, since I was dismissed? You really are illogical, aren't you?"

He was leaning back, one hand resting lightly on the wheel of the car, and his voice mocked her. This was an Angus she had never known: hard, ruthless, and displaying no chink where she could get at him. She knew what he was determined to make her do, but pride and the still painful memories of the past choked her. She blinked away the tears that unexpectedly had replaced her anger.

"Why are you so hard on me? Don't tell me you're just meeting my wishes. You're angry. Really angry with me."

"I like honesty in human relations, Linda. It's what I always liked about you when you were a kid, and afterwards. But you're not being honest now, either with yourself or with me. Your stubborn, stiff-necked pride won't let you be honest. Well, I'm not going to salvage that for you. If you can't be honest with me, then there's an end of things between us. When I left you that day, I called you a liar. I've seen nothing to make me change my opinion."

"If I climb down, what then?"

"I said then that we'd fight it out. But it'll be fought honestly, or not at all. It's up to you."

"All right," she said shakily. "I'm sorry for the things I said that day. Although they felt true at the time, I've found out that they're not. I was wrong about your grandfather and your aunt, and I don't want to be a stranger to you. I'm sorry I sent your present back, too."

"I should think so. A petty, spiteful little gesture that was. And not a word with it! All right, Lindey. That wasn't a bad effort at hauling your flag down."

"It doesn't put everything right, though."

"I know. When I said fight it out, perhaps it would have been more accurate to say try to understand how things went so wrong between us. I seem to have managed to hurt you far more than I realised and we've been at cross purposes ever since, making havoc of our friendship. I couldn't see why you should have forgiven the old man and melted into the arms of the family while finding it quite impossible to forgive me for the same crime of believing that case against you. I asked you to come back, and got a flea in my ear. Aunt Harriet asked you, and you came like a lamb."

"She told me things about your grandfather, about the past, that made me understand him better, and realise just how hard Peter Holmfield's picture of me had hit him, so that his harshness was excusable."

"What things?"

"About him and my mother. He loved her so much. In a way, I stood for her. Aunt Harriet hasn't told you, then?"

"No. Oh, I knew Grandfather was fond of your mother. I always knew her as Aunt Diana, an old friend of the family. If I hadn't grown up with it, I suppose I might have guessed. Tell me about it."

She did so, and he remained silent for a few moments after she had finished. Then he said gently:

"I always did say he was a hopeless romantic at heart. And so are you, it seems, to have been so melted. Poor old boy. He'd never have left his wife and children, of course. Divorce isn't in his code. Then to miss the chance of marrying your mother by so narrow a margin. And now he dotes on you, her daughter. Shockingly bad for you, all this indulgence. No wonder I've found you so difficult."

"*You've* found *me* difficult! How do you suppose I've found *you*? About as cosy as an iceberg. And this evening capped it. That was really base of you, Angus."

He smiled and ruffled her hair in the old friendly fashion.

"You asked for it. I didn't know George was likely to inflict physical damage, though. Your ankle looked bruised."

"It feels broken. So do all my toes."

"Let's have a look."

He switched on the light and she wriggled round and lifted the most painful foot on to the seat. The ankle was swollen and he ran his hand over it.

"You'll walk again," he said cheerfully. "Put a cold compress on it. That's a fatal ladder in your stocking, though. Justice demands that I buy you another pair. Size?"

"Nine."

"Right. You look tired, Lindey. No more inquests. Can you get your shoes on again?"

She tried and winced.

"I'll carry them."

"Gravel is not the most comfortable surface to walk on in stockinged feet. Hang on while I open the door and I'll carry you."

He lifted her easily. In his arms, she felt suddenly emotionally exhausted. She had been fighting him in her heart and her mind ever since she had left Bermuda. Now, in this moment of time when she had yielded to him, she was conscious only of a tired peace, of landfall after stormy seas. There were still issues to be settled, she was still not certain of his heart, but just then nothing mattered. His arms were strong and she was tired.

He kissed her gently after he put her down.

"Goodnight, Lindey Lou. You look all eyes. Up to bed with you."

A child still in his eyes? Perhaps. She smiled at him and went upstairs, holding her shoes in her hand, while he watched her.

22

Alliance

"ANGUS, I've a favour to ask," said Harriet, nailing her nephew in the drawing-room that Sunday morning.

"I wince, but go on."

"Will you give a hand at the school fête next Saturday? There's no home cricket match, I know."

"You cut the ground from under my feet. And what is your worthy Philip raising funds for now?"

"He is not my Philip," said Harriet severely. "You know that your grandfather and I have always taken an interest in the school."

"You don't have to make excuses, dear aunt," said Angus with a maddening smile.

"You're in a very frivolous mood this morning, young man. The fête's in aid of new equipment for the gym, and we need some help in erecting two tents in the grounds and with other odd jobs. Linda's promised to help. Will you?"

"Who am I to hinder little boys from getting some instrument of torture for their gym? I well remember the horrors of parallel bars. Why should they be spared?"

"You'll come, then?"

"At your service, Aunt Harriet. I hope Philip appreciates your loyal support. As a matter of fact, I think he does. You play a big part behind the scenes these days, don't you? Linda tells me you're doing some private coaching."

"Yes. I enjoy it. Keeps me from getting rusty. Besides, I rather like small boys, in modest doses. I always rather liked you when you were small."

"No longer, alas?"

"If you're fishing for compliments, you're in the wrong river, my boy."

"Don't I know it!" he said, grinning and putting an arm round his aunt's thin shoulders.

"The atmosphere at breakfast was decidedly more cordial between you and Linda this morning. Made it up?"

"Sort of."

"She's a dear girl, Angus. We've grown very fond of her."

"That is obvious," he said a shade drily.

"You sound disapproving."

"On the contrary. The atmosphere here at Hartfield is amazingly changed. I'm glad. I'd never have thought it possible."

"Nor I. The only jarring note was between you and Linda at the week-ends. I'm glad you've stopped sparring. You're a little intolerant, you know, Angus. Linda's an exceptionally nice person."

"I know. As well as an angel of light, she can also be a prickly young creature with the pride of the devil and a regular paddy. She may look like her mother, but she takes after her father in many ways. I liked him. He was a great naturalist. But he was easily offended and could be fiery, I remember."

"Sensitive people are often the possessors of a fierce pride. Especially if they feel failures. Stuart was a failure in his profession of letters. They were desperately poor. Those things are apt to give people an inferiority complex so that they fall back on pride and are apt to resent anything that smacks of patronage. It's foolish, but understandable."

"And should be spanked out of people while they're young."

"Or soothed away by loving."

"And there speaks one who could administer a good spanking in her day. You're growing soft and sentimental, Aunt Harriet. There's something very insidious about the honey that abounds at Hartfield these days. I've always admired your sharp mind. Don't disillusion me."

"You deserved all your spanking and more. I fancy life has spanked Linda Dawley often enough."

"What are you really trying to say?" asked Angus, his head on one side like an enquiring bird, his intelligent black eyes sizing her up.

"Don't hurt her, Angus. I think you could."

"You brood too much," he said, and patted her on the shoulder as he went out.

Which was tantamount to saying mind your own business, thought Harriet, and she had asked for it. He was an engaging young man. If she were young, she could easily fall in love with such a man: good-looking, assured, a voice that could charm a dog from his bone and a certain magnetism about his personality impossible to pin down but a potent force. Strong-willed and masterful, like his grandfather. Angus had a razor-sharp mind while his grandfather possessed more of a dogged intelligence, but the likeness was there: and such men were not easy propositions for women. Angus had a saving sense of humour which his grandfather lacked, and that, of course, could make a lot of difference. From the window, she watched him stroll across the lawn to join Linda and his grandfather. Yes, she thought, an engaging threat to any girl's peace of mind.

"Checkmate," said Luke. "You made that inevitable three moves back, my dear. Let's go back to where we were then and I'll show you."

Luke proceeded to show Linda how she could have forestalled him.

"It's no use, I'll never learn to look ahead far enough to be a good chess player."

"You're too impetuous, but you're coming on. You look a bit tired today, dear. Late night, I suppose. Did you enjoy the dance?"

"It was a great success. I discovered that

George Lyall is a much better cricketer than a dancer, though."

"H'm. Angus look after you?"

"Most efficiently," said Linda demurely.

"Good of the boy to come down every week-end. He's still working in the study, I suppose?"

"Yes. He brought a pile of work down with him this weekend."

"He's got a practice that keeps him very busy. First-class at his job. Pity he chose the profession. He'd have been brilliant in commerce. He sorted out the hotel business—gave me a crystal-clear picture of its finances and what needed to be done. Should have consulted him about it years ago. I was mad with him for opting out of the family business, though. Stubborn, independent young devil. Would be his own master."

"Perhaps that's a family trait."

"What? I'd have given him his head in the business, up to a point. Well, it's an old story now. Ours hasn't been a very happy family history, my dear. When my son married again — Angus took that hard. Never liked his stepmother or her son. Well, perhaps he was a better judge than

I. It was a great shock to me, Cynthia's two-faced handling of that affair. But we'll not talk of that."

Linda stacked the chess-men away in their box. Luke leaned back in his chair, his craggy old face parchment-coloured under the light. He closed his eyes and she thought he had dropped off to sleep until he said:

"You know, in a way, Diana, my money's been at the root of much of the family trouble. Cynthia and Roland after it. I realise that now. And because Angus knew of his stepmother's obsession about the money, it made him touchy about it. Well, nobody could accuse him of sucking up to me for money—a thorny trial he was to me. He's all right, though. A man of integrity. Our old rows don't matter any more. He wants me to leave my money to charity, you know, after providing for Harriet and his father so that there's no real hardship. Suggested I did it while I was alive and save estate duty. We had a long talk. Never felt so close to the boy. Think his scruples about my money foolish, of course. Independence is all very fine, but blood's thicker than water and he's a

Ferndale. Told him I thought his suggestion was sound, though. And so I did."

Linda went quietly to the window to draw the curtains, for moths were coming in and fluttering round the light, but her movement seemed to draw Luke back to the present. He opened his eyes, blinked and said:

"That was a good game, my dear. Thank you."

"I enjoyed it. I must try to get a few tips from Angus on the quiet and see if I can beat you just once more. It's time for your pills, isn't it?"

He eyed the green tablets which she brought him with a wry look that reminded her of Angus.

"The modern witchcraft. Oh well, I suppose it pleases our new young doctor. He doesn't know half as much as old Doctor Gretty for all his up-to-date techniques. The new scientists may be clever, but they're not often wise, my dear. And a good doctor needs to be both. You do me more good than any pills. It's odd to think that in many ways these are the happiest days I've ever known. Read a few pages to me, dear, before I go to bed."

They had started *David Copperfield*, and Linda was reading it when Angus came in. He signalled to her to go on, and sat in the armchair opposite her while she continued to narrate the circumstances of David Copperfield's adoption by his aunt. At the close of the chapter, he observed with a faint smile:

"Betsey Trotwood was always my favourite character in that book. Aunt Harriet has distinct affinities with her."

"Harriet? Where is your aunt?" demanded Luke. "Haven't seen her all the evening."

"She went to have a conference with Philip Hanwood about next Saturday's junketings."

"She didn't say. Well, I'm for bed. Just ring for Stevens, dear, will you?"

When he had gone, Linda said:

"Have you finished your work, Angus?"

"Yes. Haven't had a chance to be alone with you all day. Grandfather monopolises you, doesn't he?"

"Not altogether. I have my mornings free for work in the week. I don't grudge him the rest of the time. We're happy together."

"It's a nice night. Care for a stroll?"

She fetched her coat and they walked across the lawn and along the path between the borders. The moon was nearly full and in its pale light the white chalices of some lilies stood out like pale, beautiful ghosts. Linda stooped to smell one, and decided that its fragrance was almost too strong at such close quarters and that she preferred the lighter scent of some tobacco plants at the end of the border. Angus put an arm round her shoulders when they sat down on the seat by the pool.

"It seems a long time ago—that evening when we last sat here together. Remember?" he asked.

"Yes. A lot's happened since then. I feel a different person."

"You were uncertain of yourself. A bit shy and awkward. Scarcely a word to say for yourself when the others were around. Watching you with Grandfather now— things certainly have changed. You're a good giver, Linda, but a bad taker, aren't you?"

She thought for a moment, then said:

"I suppose I am. It's been rather like King Cophetua and the beggar maid, and

. . . I saw an element of humiliation in it. I was raw."

"But not now—with Grandfather and Aunt Harriet."

"They've given me love, too, this time."

He was a few moments digesting this, then went on:

"And getting your book accepted. That's helped the inferiority complex quite a bit, I guess."

"I still can't quite believe it. Have I been looking like a proud parent?"

"As far as I'm concerned, more like an angry teacher, but Aunt Harriet said that when the proofs of your book arrived this week you carried them round to show everybody as though showing off your medals."

"I'll come down to earth," she said, smiling. "I've only a small talent and I don't expect any more success than my father had, but it's my own work that someone wants to print for children to read. That pleases me a lot. I shall send a copy to Sandra and John Lock, who gave me the idea for the book. I dedicated it to them; I thought it would please them."

"Sandra and John Lock?"

"The children I brought home from Bermuda."

"Ah yes. When you bolted. And why was it so much harder to forgive me, Linda? I stood up for you as far as I could at that showdown, but the evidence was overwhelming, and I had as good a reason as my grandfather for being angry. We were friends. You'd promised to keep me informed. I arrived in Bermuda looking forward to carrying on where we left off, only to find, as seemed clear, that you'd been carrying on an affair with Peter Holmfield from the moment I left. Could you reasonably expect me to be kind?"

"Perhaps not. But I'd sooner you'd thought me downright wicked than a silly creature whose head was liable to be turned by any man. You seemed more annoyed because I'd given your stepmother the victory she wanted than for any other reason. I was written off as an inexperienced girl bowled over by moonlight, blue lagoons and the sudden proximity of men. And you were my friend, I thought. I found your picture of me more insulting than your grandfather's. And I still do."

"Your pride makes you think that you

should never be suspected of human frailty, does it?"

"If the positions had been reversed, and I'd thought that of you, how would you have felt?"

"Damned angry. But my first target would have been the party who'd fixed it on me. I shouldn't have bolted, all injured pride, determined to have nothing more to do with any of the players in that little melodrama. Nor should I have hidden myself in a bolt-hole. I'd have ferreted out the truth, then accepted the apologies. If you'd hammered Holmfield, he'd have yielded the truth. He didn't want to get you into trouble. You were being unrealistic in expecting people to believe you in the face of that evidence. I shouldn't have expected it."

"Not of your friends, if you denied it?"

"I doubt it."

"I would have believed you if you'd denied it, whatever the evidence."

That silenced him for a moment, then he took her hand and said:

"You're an idealist, Linda. I'm a realist. If you expect so much, I'm almost bound to hurt you. That picture I drew wasn't insulting; it was the most likely explanation I could find in the light of my knowledge of you and of human desire. That night in Bermuda after the dance: it only needed a spark and we'd have gone up. You knew it and I knew it. Do you deny it?"

"No."

"Well, then, I had to leave you there, a young, attractive, inexperienced girl, ripe for love, surrounded by everything conducive to it. Was it so inconceivable—my version? Come down from that lofty plane and remember that you're made of flesh and blood like the rest of us."

"You make me sound such a prig. But it hurt, so much. And that night with you . . . it was different. It wasn't just a physical thing. There was more to it."

"At the time I thought so, too. But your letters gave nothing away. They were factual, but revealed absolutely nothing about your feelings. When I heard the Holmfield story, I told myself that was the reason why."

"I felt afraid to reveal too much. You'd been warning me against losing my heart. You'd offered me friendship. I didn't want to frighten that off."

"Well, where do we go from here, Lindey? I thought, when your present came back, well that's that. Put her out of your mind. If she's got such an outsize chip on her shoulder, she's better forgotten. But I couldn't forget. When I saw you coming along the lane with Harriet that day, I could have throttled you or beaten you, but I knew I couldn't forget you. And I knew from your face that even if you had given me the push in no uncertain fashion some weeks before, you'd not forgotten me, either."

"And that was when you ungallantly sized me up and decided that you'd make me crawl before you'd talk to me again."

"Not crawl. Just haul down that pride of yours."

"You speak as though it's all me, but isn't it a case of the pot calling the kettle black? You've all the Ferndale arrogance, you know."

"But I'm not an idealist as well. That's a fatal combination. I wouldn't want to hurt you, Lindey, and that's why I'm talking so much instead of doing what I most want to do, and that's take you in my arms and be done with words. I know if I did, all the arguments would stop, but underneath they'd still be there, to be lived with. I could sweep you off your feet and be swept off myself; God knows it would be easy. But have we the right temperaments to live happily together? I've seen enough of unhappy marriages to make me wary. People can damage each other so much, and I'd hate to damage you."

"I had no doubts when I was waiting for you to come again to Bermuda. If you love me, I've none now."

"The idealist? Well, it's certainly done the trick with Grandfather. But is the old family feud really dead in your heart, Linda? The old man's sick and helpless now, and appeals to your compassion. But if he was still strong and active and domineering, as he was? I think, deep inside you, your father instilled some of his dislike of us. You've seen me as patronising. I may have been lots of objectionable things, but I've never been guilty of patronising you. I wanted to protect you: that's different. You saw the old man as a patron, but he was doing what he did out of love for your mother. When you told me what you thought of the Ferndales, I felt that you were almost glad to have your father's opinion justified. Are you really free of that resentment, or shall I have it dished up to me in future when we have rows? Too much pride and independence, and the old family feud between us: are we going to be happy together?"

"The old feud is over and done with, now that I know you all better. My father had reason to be bitter. I have none. Perhaps it needed that horrible business in Bermuda to blow everything up so that we could all start again, understanding each other better."

"Perhaps. You were very fond of your father, weren't you?"

"Yes. He was too sensitive a person to thrive on adversity, though. He felt a failure. And although our home life when Mother was alive was happy enough, I think he must have guessed about her and your grandfather, don't you?"

"Sensed it, yes. I don't see how it could be otherwise. He wasn't obtuse in any way."

"Mother used to treat him like a child, you know. She was always lively and affectionate with both of us. But it probably added to his sense of failure."

"And in a specially bitter way. I had a taste of what it felt like when I thought you were in love with Holmfield, and, unlike your father, I didn't even have any claim on you."

"But you went out to the party at Roland's bungalow that evening."

"I felt too savage to trust myself with you any more that day. And in the morning, the bird had flown. I spent weeks trying to track you down but I couldn't get hold of a single clue. If it hadn't been for that advertisement of yours, I might still be looking."

"Did you still want to know me, believing the scandal about me to be true, then?"

"I felt in an odd way responsible for you. I have, ever since you came back into our lives after your father died. And I still do. So make up your mind. If you marry me, you'll be taken charge of. I can't stop it. Perhaps it dates from our childhood. Going to put up with it?"

He was teasing her now, but underneath she sensed that he was warning her.

"I have my methods," she said demurely.

"You have, too. Look at the way Grandfather eats out of your hand now. I'm the one who should be scared. I'll be in the web, ensnared by a pair of soft brown eyes, still thinking I'm master when in fact I'll be trussed up with your silk thread."

"That will be the day."

"Why are we wasting time, blathering like this? Love me, Lindey Lou?"

"Yes."

He kissed her then and pulled her into his lap. Sliding his arm under her coat, he held her close. A bat swooped by, unnoticed, and an owl hooted from the distance. She moved her hand through his thick black hair and felt she was entering an entirely new, enchanting, intoxicating country.

They were brought back to familiar country by a low growl, then the old mastiff, recognising them, walked slowly up and put his head on Linda's lap. Harriet, hesitating by a rhododendron bush, said:

"No use pretending I'm not here, since Jason has decided to intrude."

"Hullo, Aunt Harriet," said Angus cheerfully, waving a friendly hand to the seat. "Come and join us. It's a lovely night."

"I'm too old to enjoy a chilly seat in the moonlight."

"It's really quite warm," said Linda, held fast by her imperturbable lover, who gave a chuckle at this naïve remark.

"Jason and I don't warm up so easily," said Harriet drily.

"Come on, Aunt Harriet. Relax and give us your blessing. Linda and I have cast caution to the winds and are going to be married. That's what the moonlight has done to us. So stop hovering like a forbidding wraith and join us. I'll lend you an arm to keep you warm."

"My dear children," said Harriet, sitting beside them, "I'm delighted. As an elderly spinster, I can't claim to be an authority on marriage, but I think you two have a reasonable chance of making a good thing of it. I wish you both the greatest happiness. There hasn't been too much going round in this family. It seems a bit overdue."

"Thank you," said Angus. "I'm

315

relieved, after your grim warning to me this morning, that you sound so optimistic."

"I was afraid you might be amusing yourself."

"What? How could you?" said Angus wickedly.

"It wouldn't be without precedent, young man. I seem to remember a procession of playthings in the past."

"So do I," said Linda. "And they were always pretty ones."

"Have mercy. I can't take on the two of you. I had my fun in my salad days, and all parties enjoyed it, but I've put away childish things for some time now, and I've always taken this party seriously. Deny it if you can, madam."

"I can't. You were my mentor, right from the start," said Linda.

"Well, you two may be impervious to chills, but I'm not. And nor is Jason. He's stiff with rheumatism as it is, poor old chap. If you can tear yourselves away from the moonlight, I think we might have a bottle of champagne to celebrate before we go to bed."

"Good idea. All this talk of chills and

rheumatism has broken the spell, anyway," said Angus, swinging Linda to her feet.

Their high spirits coupled with the champagne broke down Harriet's customary reserve and she toasted them with a greater show of feeling than either of them had seen in her before.

"Angus," she said, "has always been dear to me, in spite of being quite the most unmanageable boy I ever came across, and Linda has become equally dear to me these last months, so to see you marry and to have Linda brought into the family gives me the greatest joy and satisfaction. There's something about the Dawley women that seems necessary to the Ferndale men, and I'm truly glad that in this case, the two have come together. Long years of happiness to you both, my dears."

"Thank you, Aunt Harriet," said Angus, drawing Linda to him. "I know I'm a lucky man, and I'll do my best to see that Linda never regrets being a Ferndale. Do you think Grandfather will be pleased?"

"Overjoyed, I'm sure. You've no doubts on that score, have you?"

"Not really. It occurred to me that he

won't want to give her up, though, even to me."

"Well, you're not proposing to elope tomorrow, are you?"

"No. But I don't want a long engagement."

"I've promised him the summer, Angus," said Linda.

"All right. But we'll be married in the autumn. Agreed?"

"For a man who only proposed an hour ago, you work very fast, darling," said Linda.

"You haven't answered the question."

Harriet saw their eyes meet and wondered whether this was to be the first battle between sense and sensibility.

"Darling, you know I would gladly marry you tomorrow, but your grandfather depends so much on me now."

"You were going to leave Hartfield at the end of the summer anyway, I understood."

"That was what I originally intended, but I've realised lately that it would be cruel to leave him. He can hardly bear me out of his sight now."

"I know. It's becoming obsessive and you must draw a line. We'll be living in

London at first, but we'll still be able to come down here to see him at the week-ends. That's a reasonable proposition. So, the beginning of October at the latest, Linda?"

For a moment, Harriet thought Linda was going to argue. The struggle in the girl's face was obvious. Angus was right. Linda had become an obsession with the old man. He was reliving his past with her. But he could not be allowed to monopolise her life indefinitely. Linda, sensitive and moved by his frustrated love for her mother, was too tender of heart to leave him now, for all her early intentions to remain free. People like Linda could never be free, thought Harriet. Loving hearts were always bound. Torn now between her love for Angus and her compassion for the old man, she looked appealingly at Angus, but he was putting her to the test and he waited, his eyes holding hers, and suddenly she gave in.

"Very well, my lord," she said, putting her hand in his.

Relieved at that victory of rational thought over sentiment, Harriet said briskly:

"You're just guessing that Father won't want Linda to leave him. He may be so pleased to see her marry into the family that he'll put up with seeing rather less of her."

"If I know Grandfather, he'll want to have his cake and eat it. A nice long engagement is what he'll plump for. The leopard doesn't change his spots, you know, illness or not," said Angus.

"Do you have to return to London first thing in the morning?" asked Harriet. "Couldn't you stay and see your grandfather before you go?"

"Yes. I'll ring the office in the morning. In fact, to savour the pleasures of being engaged, I'll take the day off and go back to London in the evening. That will give us all time to get future plans settled."

"You seem to have got them settled, darling," said Linda.

"I was thinking of the other parties," said Angus blandly.

"Well, for a pair heading for matrimony, you two have been cutting some odd capers over the past weeks. Perhaps I'm old-fashioned, though, and this is the contemporary style of wooing," said Harriet.

"No sentimentality," said Angus, grinning. "I leave that to Grandfather. I just had to crack Linda."

"How very uncomfortable for her. Well, I'm for bed, and so should you be. It's nearly one o'clock."

"In a few minutes," said Angus, and Harriet left them.

Angus took Linda by the shoulders and held her firmly at arm's length. His eyes surveyed her from head to toe with an expression that brought the colour to her cheeks.

"You belong to me now, Linda. Let there be no mistake about that. You've committed yourself, and I won't share. You don't want to retract?"

"No, my love," she said with a tenderness that softened his expression, and she went into his arms to give him the reassurance he needed.

23

Estate matters

"WELL, Angus," said Luke, surveying his grandson with his shrewd grey eyes, "you've done a lot of things I haven't approved of, but in this decision, the most important of your life, my boy, you've delighted me. I congratulate you on your good sense. But how long's this been brewing? I had no idea. Didn't think you two hit it off too well, as a matter of fact."

"We had a few difficulties to iron out. I'm glad you approve, Grandfather. We're going to be married at the beginning of October."

"What's that? October? Why all the rush? Plenty of time."

"None to waste," said Angus lightly.

"Nonsense. All your lives in front of you. Can't rush Linda off her feet like this. She'll want to think about the sort of home she wants, plan it. Not easy to find a decent house these days. It's not a holiday you're proposing. What a precipitate chap you are, Angus!"

"We can live at my flat to start with, and come down here at week-ends to do some house-hunting. Linda likes the country, and we'll have to find somewhere with a reasonable journey up to London, but that can all wait until we're married."

"A cock-eyed way of doing things. I shan't agree. Linda, my dear, you mustn't let him rush you off your feet like this. You'll want time to plan the future. You must stay here at Hartfield and we can take our time looking for the right house for you. You'll need at least a year. I'll get Dakers on the job. He's a good agent. Somewhere in Surrey or Sussex should suit."

"Dear Uncle Luke," said Linda, taking his hand, "we shall be coming down every week-end, and I'll come down in the week, too, if I can manage it, but we want to be married in the autumn."

"But. . . but, confound it, weddings take a lot of planning. I'm not going to have a hole-in-the-corner affair for you. There's the family to get over from Bermuda. No, it's all too precipitate."

Angus put his arm round Linda's shoulder as they stood there, by Luke's bedside, and said quietly:

"We're in love, Grandfather, and we're going to be married quietly at the beginning of October. I know you're very fond of Linda, and as my wife, she'll belong to the family always. Surely that can't take place quickly enough for you. It can't for me."

"You young people — always in such a hurry. You want to be married in the autumn, Linda?"

"Yes, dear."

"Well, I know Angus too well to think he'll be persuaded by me. I've not long to go now. Perhaps it would be as well to see you made Mrs. Ferndale in the autumn. But I'll not agree to some poky wedding in a registrar's office, if that's what you mean by a quiet wedding, Angus. Our name stands for something in Edenmere, and the union of a Dawley with a Ferndale shall be celebrated properly in our church," said Luke, glaring angrily at his grandson.

Angus, willing to concede a point, having won the battle, said with a smile:

324

"Very well, Grandfather. You and Linda shall plan that as you wish."

"We'll discuss it with Harriet today. She's a good organiser. We've not much more than three months. Always impatient and set on getting your own way, Angus. I hope you'll look after my little girl well. She's a treasure, you know."

"I do know. And I'll look after her, I promise you."

"H'm. Well, in spite of deploring the rush, I'm very pleased with you over this, Angus. Began to think you'd never marry and settle down. A happy marriage is the greatest help and blessing a man can have, and the influence of a fine girl like Linda will be of enormous benefit to you. I've always said. . ."

Angus's mouth twitched as his grandfather embarked on the theme which he had played so often to him in the past, but he listened patiently and then said:

"I agree with every word, Grandfather, which is why I'm so anxious to benefit just as soon as possible."

The old man acknowledged this scoring point with a grim smile, and Linda stooped and kissed him for conceding the battle so much more gallantly than she had feared.

To everybody's amazement, Luke Ferndale seemed to take on a new lease of life after the engagement. Instead of living so much in the past, his mind regained much of its old vigour and occupied itself with the present and the future which he had believed he would never see. He not only took an active part in planning the wedding, but decided to put into operation Angus's scheme to set up a charity trust, of which he would be head. Summoning Angus to a discussion one week-end in July, they thrashed out the details.

"I saw Rainwood yesterday," said Luke, "and gave him instructions to draw up a new will. I've appointed you and him joint executors. He's a sound chap, Rainwood. As good as his father was, and that's saying a lot. I want you to know how I've disposed of my estate, Angus. Then we won't discuss it again. I've decided to use half of my money on this charity trust of yours."

"Splendid."

"The rest I've disposed of as follows. I've looked after the staff—Amos, the Martins and so on—so that they'll have a comfortable old age. After that, one sixth of the remainder of my estate will go to your father, one sixth to your aunt Harriet, one third to you and one third to Linda."

Angus was silent for a moment, then said: "It's very generous of you, Grandfather, but you know I . . ."

"Yes, yes, I know your scruples, but now you're getting married and your children will be Ferndales, you need to think differently. You're the only one to carry on our family, and I feel a duty to the family name. And to Diana's daughter. You don't know how much this marriage means to me, my boy. It seems to have opened up the future in a way I never expected."

"I might say the same, and I owe it to you, Grandfather, that Linda was brought within my reach at all. For that, I shall be eternally grateful. Now, do you wish me to keep what you've told me to myself, or may I tell Linda?"

"You may. And your aunt. Nobody else. And I don't wish to talk about the will any more. Now about this charity trust. I shall have a small committee of trustees consisting of you, Rainwood, and possibly Harriet. What do you think?"

"Certainly Aunt Harriet. She's very practical and she'll cope with the administration side admirably."

"Right. I shall be chairman and decide which causes to support, but I shall welcome suggestions. I want to use the money for the benefit of our own neighbourhood of Edenmere and for the individual needs and enterprises of its inhabitants. I shall examine each cause carefully, with your help, of course, and I shall favour helping handicapped people who are doing their best to help themselves, and contributing to any worthwhile community need."

"Excellent. I'll work out the constitution this week," said Angus, delighted at the renewed grip the old man had on life.

When they had finished discussing the details, Luke pulled out his watch and said:

"Now I must go. Just wheel me back to my room. The physiotherapist is due in five minutes. I've told him I intend to walk down the aisle to give Linda away. Refuse to spoil the occasion with a wheel-chair. So there's some hard work to be done. If you'd given me longer, Angus, it would have helped, of course."

"You'll do it, if you've set your mind on it," said Angus cheerfully as he guided the chair through the door.

Looking for Linda, he found her grooming Jason on the lawn. He stood on the terrace watching her, unnoticed. She was wearing a short-sleeved, cream-colour dress, simply cut and of a silky material that showed the slender, graceful lines of her figure. The sunshine brought out the coppery tinge in her brown hair, and her diamond engagement ring flashed as her hand wielded the brush with long, firm sweeps over Jason's broad back. Absorbed in her task, she lifted up his head next and did his chest. The old dog stood like a statue, his hindquarters drooping a little, for age was leaving its mark. Then she put the brush down and cupped the grey muzzle in her hands, murmuring some endearment, and the tenderness of her expression struck home to Angus with moving impact. He had seen it often before: with his grandfather, with an injured fledgeling blackbird, with any living creature that was weak or old or

329

young and helpless. She had been the same when she was a child—too sensitive for her own comfort and too tenderhearted for this rough world, which was why she had always aroused his protective instincts. It made her unduly vulnerable. He had forgotten that in the angry heat of the events in Bermuda, and had underestimated the hurt he had inflicted. He would never forget it again. And when, after he had been making love to her, he caught that same tenderness for him in her face, it never failed to move him and give his love a dimension too deep for words.

As Jason slowly wagged his tail at Linda's endearments, she looked up and smiled as she saw Angus.

"You make a delectable kennel-maid," he said going across to her and kissing her. "Jason is lucky. Come for a walk. I want you to myself for a bit."

They went arm in arm through the woodland and down to the stream. He told her about his grandfather's will and the charity trust.

"You never wanted to inherit it, did you? Do you mind now?" she asked, her head on one side.

"Well, as Grandfather pointed out, I'm founding a family now. I was so sickened by my stepmother's predatory aims that I wanted none of it. She and Roland are in for a disappointment and I don't weep over that. Anyway, I'm glad the old man's decided to use half of his money for this charity trust. It'll give him an interest. I may say that it will have to be a very deserving cause to win Grandfather's support, and no professional cadgers will stand a chance. You know his principles: hard work, thrift, self-help before all. He'll investigate all causes with the utmost thoroughness, if I know him. I really think this will give him something to bite on. It's what he needs. And Aunt Harriet will get a lot of satisfaction and interest out of it, too. I bet she'll be grinding an axe for the prep school."

"I admire her. She's given her life to standing by your grandfather, and yet she's never lost her independent spirit, nor been embittered because Uncle Luke has taken it all for granted. Do you think she and Philip Hanwood might come together?"

"It's a friendship she values. And she's keenly interested in the school. I've seen a difference in her these past years since she's taken such a big part in helping Philip behind the scenes. She's been happier, I think, though she never parades her feelings. But if it's marriage you're thinking of. . . I very much doubt it, although your guess is as good as mine. Somehow I think Aunt Harriet's a determined spinster now, though."

"I always found her forbidding when I was young. But underneath, she has a generous heart. I've grown very fond of her."

"I'm glad. I've always liked her. I wonder whether my father will come over for the wedding. I bet my stepmother and her contingent won't. They'll be furious about it. My father may come. He won't want to upset the old man, although when he came over in March, when we thought Grandfather was dying, he was still angry at the letter the old man had sent to Cynthia apropos your affair. It was apparently a snorter."

"All that seems like a bad dream now, but I suppose it was Enid Holmfield who was most to blame. A bit unlucky for your stepmother, perhaps, the way it turned out."

"Nonsense, my dear. She engineered that showdown. Holmfield's letter made that clear. Grandfather wrote and pressed him for exact details of my stepmother's part, you know, and Holmfield's reply left no doubt that she had deliberately led you forward as a scapegoat with the assurance that she'd make light of it and no harm would come to you. And she added some more strokes to blacken your character at the bungalow that evening. Very regretfully, of course. Grandfather has a keen memory, and although he's always been blinded by my stepmother's charm and good looks, he doesn't have wool pulled over his eyes more than once. I think it's just because he has that romantic, chivalrous attitude to women, especially pretty women, that he was so shocked and angry to discover the malice behind it. In some ways, he's like an adolescent."

"What a good thing his grandson is hard-headed and no romantic," said Linda, smiling.

"It is. And don't think I'm going to spoil you like he does, young woman. Talk about maudlin indulgence! It's a fantasy world he's been living in with you. Moonlight and roses and late larks singing."

"Who was it I was with under the moon last night? And didn't I hear some heart-stirring words then, too?"

"That was no fantasy. That was splendid reality," said Angus, grinning. "Anyway, I rather like the late lark singing theme of Grandfather's. Some truth there, I guess."

They had reached the stone bridge, and lingered there, remembering.

"You were disappointed in me that day, when you hauled me up," she said. "I could sense it."

"You'd lost your sparkle. Seemed a bit dimmer than I remembered. You soon corrected that, though."

"I'd been driven into my shell by so much solitude, I suppose. You seemed to me just as challenging, and likeable, and exasperating as ever. And I think I knew, deep down inside me, as soon as I looked up from the stream and saw you. Susceptible, you see," she added, laughing at him. "Liable to lose her head immediately. Just as you said."

"You've been getting considerable enjoyment lately from the objectionable habit of throwing up my own words to confound me. Well, I'm not going to eat them, and I shall extract a forfeit from you every time you do it."

It was some moments before he released her, saying: "Happy?"

"So happy that I'm almost afraid."

"That's foolish. To reassure you, let's get back to practical matters. Robert Rainwood, Grandfather's solicitor, telephoned me to let me know that a friend of his was selling his house at Lynwood. The old man had told him we were looking for a house in this part of Surrey. It sounded rather a nice proposition. A couple of acres of ground. Handy for the station. Not on the market yet. I said we'd like to have a look at it. If you agree, I'll telephone and make an appointment this week-end if I can."

"Do. Lynwood would be ideal."

Excitedly, she plied him with questions and they walked back along the stream, making plans for the future which to both of them promised so much.

"If this is the home we're looking for, it will make it seem really true. Sometimes I still can't believe that we shall be married before the leaves fall from these trees," she said.

"In ten weeks precisely, you will be driving to church in your wedding dress to be given away by Grandfather in the presence of the whole village, it seems, and heaven knows who else, for Aunt Harriet says she can't put a curb on Grandfather. One might think it was his wedding. And he's going to walk down the aisle if it kills him."

"I think, in a way, it *is* his wedding."

"Yes. Well, even if we'd have preferred something quieter, we'll not grudge him his pleasure in telling the world. Hope it's a day like this," said Angus.

24

Trysting-place

THE day dawned mistily, but the sun had broken through by the middle of the morning and Luke felt it warm on his face as he stood in the porch waiting for Linda. When she came, he stood looking at her with pride and affection in his eyes and a jaw grimly set to control the emotion he felt. The classic line of her white satin dress, with its fitted bodice, long sleeves and sweeping skirt, was timeless, and Linda carried it off with the elegance of a bygone age, reminding him more than ever of Diana. She wore her mother's pearls and carried a bouquet of white roses.

"Well, Uncle Luke, the sun is shining for us," she said, smiling.

"A beautiful bride, my dear. And a happy one. That's plain to see. The sun wouldn't dare not to shine today. Now, Martin, help Miss Linda into the car."

Slowly, with the aid of his stick, Luke followed her and was helped into the car. Impeccable in morning dress, he showed no signs of strain, aware of Linda's eyes watching him a little anxiously. Indomitably, he had made himself walk again, first with the aid of a frame, then with two sticks, and for the past two weeks with the aid of only one stick. One leg dragged and he had to walk slowly, but he was able to hold himself upright with no signs of instability, and was irritated by too eager offers of help.

"Not nervous?" he asked gruffly as Linda laid her hand on his for a moment.

"Not a bit. Too happy to be nervous."

"That's good. This is your day, dear. A day to remember all your life."

The first leaves were falling from the ash tree on the corner of the lane, and in the hedgerow the hawthorn berries were red and thick. Along the sunken lane, the beeches overhead showed the first tinge of yellow. It was at this time of the year, thought Luke, that her mother had married that Dawley fellow. He remembered it so

338

clearly: a gusty, showery day. Diana, beyond the age for a white wedding, had worn a coat the colour of chartreuse with a little velvet hat that matched. She had always had good taste in clothes, but lacked the means to indulge it after her marriage. He remembered the desolate bitterness in his heart that day as he had sat in the church beside his wife. For better, for worse. Well, he had stuck by his principles, but the irony of his freedom a few months later had seared him. They had never spoken of it except that once, he and Diana, but she had left a letter for him to be opened after her death. He had read it again last night, although he knew it by heart, before locking it away with the other mementoes he cherished. As the car swung round to the church, he roused himself and came back to the present. Today, the sun was shining and Diana's daughter was marrying his grandson, joining the Dawleys and Ferndales at last. It was a wonderfully consoling harvest.

At the entrance to the church, Linda's brown eyes met his for a moment, and they exchanged a wordless message of affection and confidence, then she laid her hand lightly on his right arm, and slowly they began their journey down the aisle to the soft music of Purcell. The two small bridesmaids, nieces of Philip Hanwood, followed with faces solemn with concentration.

Harriet, a little anxious for her father, was glad when his clear and firm "I do" in response to the question "Who giveth this woman to this man?" ended his part in the proceedings and enabled him to join her in the pew. He showed no sign of discomfort, but she noticed little beads of perspiration above his lip. She returned her gaze to the young couple at the altar. Angus looked as handsome and imperturbable as ever, and his deep voice could be heard from every seat in that small church. He looked a little paler than usual, though. Beneath that urbanity of his, his feelings ran deeper than might be guessed. Linda looked radiant, and sounded as though she was absolutely sure of what she was doing. "To love and to cherish. . ." said Angus.

When it was all over, and Linda and Angus had driven away from Hartfield to an unknown destination, and the last guests were leaving, Luke told Harriet that he would go in the car to see Austin off at Lynwood Station. His son, the only member of that branch of the family to attend the wedding, was returning to London straight away so that he could catch the first flight to Bermuda the next morning.

"I'll go. You've had a tiring day, Father," said Harriet.

"Nonsense. I feel fine. No need for you to bother.'

"I'll come, too, then."

The reason for her father's insistence on seeing his son off at the station became clear to Harriet on their way back.

"I'm stopping at Rushleigh church. Putting Linda's wedding flowers on her mother's grave," he said abruptly. "No need for you to wait. Martin can drive you home and come back for me. I shall stay a little."

"Are you sure you're not overdoing it? I can put the flowers on the grave for you."

"Don't fuss, Harriet. A little rest up there on my own for a bit will be welcome."

"Very well. But let me come and arrange

OOL23

the flowers and fetch fresh water. And you must put your coat on. Then I'll leave you, and Martin can come back in half an hour. Will that suit you?"

"All right. Austin seemed in sombre mood for a wedding guest. You'd think he'd be glad his son had married such a fine girl."

"I dare say he has domestic problems," said Harriet drily.

"Maybe. Maybe. Well, it all went off very well, Harriet."

"Yes. A happy outcome of our troubles. I must confess I never thought I'd see you walk again, Father. A triumph of mind over matter."

"I'll see a year or two yet, if God is willing. Want to get this trust on a sound footing so that you'll know how to carry out my wishes after I go. And I'd like to see another Ferndale born. A year or two, perhaps."

He had put Linda's bouquet in the boot of the car, wrapped in damp paper and polythene, and Harriet took it while Martin opened the lych-gate and gave Luke his arm to lean on as they walked up the gravel path. Rushleigh church was old and grey, with a squat tower and a Norman arch over the door. The churchyard was dominated by a fine old yew tree, and overgrown hedgerows formed its boundaries. When she had taken off the wire and arranged the white roses in the urn at the foot of Diana Dawley's grave, Harriet sat down beside her father on the seat near by. It was overhung by a silver birch tree which was shedding its leaves on the grass, and a robin was singing its piercing, plaintive autumn song from one of the branches.

Luke sat there, hunched in his coat and leaning with both hands on his stick, his face grey and lined with fatigue. He said nothing, his expression remote. He might have been carved out of stone, and Harriet knew he had forgotten her. She had taken him for a hard, unfeeling man until she had seen the love he had lavished on Linda and had learned more of the past from him when he was ill. She no longer felt bitter, as she had when she was young, because he showed her no love, and to see it poured out on a young woman who had played no part in his life until the last few months had evoked no resentment; she was fond of Linda and glad of the warmth she had brought into their lives. But it did evoke a wry irony as she looked back on her own life. If she had been pretty or charming, he might have been proud of his daughter. But she had been born a Martha, and Mary's rewards were not for her. Or perhaps it would have made no difference whatever she had been like: perhaps it was only Dawley blood to which he could respond with love. One of the consolations of growing older, she thought as she got up, was that you learned to accept things. Diana, wife of Stuart Dawley. Had her father, even now, learned to accept that without pain? Looking at him, she doubted it.

"I'll leave you now, Father. Martin will come straight back and fetch you."

"Tell him to wait at the gate. I'll come when I'm ready."

"Don't stay and get cold."

He made no reply, and she could feel him wishing her away. At the lych-gate, she turned and looked back at him. He was still leaning on his stick, motionless, gazing at the headstone of the grave, and the robin was still singing. A few more leaves drifted down as a faint wind stirred the branches of the birch tree. The sun was sinking, casting a golden glow over the quiet, deserted place. She closed the lych-gate and left the old man with his memories.

THE END

GUIDE
TO THE COLOUR CODING
OF
ULVERSCROFT BOOKS

Many of our readers have written to us expressing their appreciation for the way in which our colour coding has assisted them in selecting the Ulverscroft books of their choice. To remind everyone of our colour coding— this is as follows:

BLACK COVERS
Mysteries

★

BLUE COVERS
Romances

★

RED COVERS
Adventure Suspense and General Fiction

★

ORANGE COVERS
Westerns

★

GREEN COVERS
Non-Fiction

ROMANCE TITLES
in the
Ulverscroft Large Print Series

THE SHADOWS
OF THE CROWN TITLES
in the
Ulverscroft Large Print Series

FICTION TITLES
in the
Ulverscroft Large Print Series

MYSTERY TITLES
in the
Ulverscroft Large Print Series

Henrietta Who?	*Catherine Aird*
Slight Mourning	*Catherine Aird*
The China Governess	*Margery Allingham*
Coroner's Pidgin	*Margery Allingham*
Crime at Black Dudley	*Margery Allingham*
Look to the Lady	*Margery Allingham*
More Work for the Undertaker	
	Margery Allingham
Death in the Channel	*J. R. L. Anderson*
Death in the City	*J. R. L. Anderson*
Death on the Rocks	*J. R. L. Anderson*
A Sprig of Sea Lavender	*J. R. L. Anderson*
Death of a Poison-Tongue	*Josephine Bell*
Murder Adrift	*George Bellairs*
Strangers Among the Dead	*George Bellairs*
The Case of the Abominable Snowman	
	Nicholas Blake
The Widow's Cruise	*Nicholas Blake*
The Brides of Friedberg	*Gwendoline Butler*
Murder By Proxy	*Harry Carmichael*
Post Mortem	*Harry Carmichael*
Suicide Clause	*Harry Carmichael*
After the Funeral	*Agatha Christie*
The Body in the Library	*Agatha Christie*